RIMA RAY

Death of an Idol

Part 1 - Red

BMB
Publishing

For the idols I love—Cha Eunwoo, Hyunjin, Jungkook, Bang Chan, IU, Lisa, Jennie, BIBI, Hwasa, Sunmi, and the "Idol's Idol," Taemin.

IDOLATRY

"... the worship of someone or something other than God as though it were God."

—Encyclopedia Britannica

Contents

Preface

Death of an Idol is a psychological thriller, yes—
but it is also a love letter.

A story born from love.

My love for Korea—the country, its culture, its language, and above all, its people.

The book is set in the dazzling, high-pressure world of K-pop that emerged out of Seoul in the 1990s. Like many Americans, my first introduction to the phenomenon came in 2012 when the world became enchanted with the catchy tune and dance of PSY's "Gangnam Style." That curiosity led me to other popular groups of the time like Miss A, 2NE1, and BIGBANG.

But life took over as I immersed myself in my PhD and academic career as a professor, and K-pop drifted quietly into the background.

Years later, that spark reignited—unexpectedly—through my introduction to webtoons or manhwas: Korean comics similar in vein to Japanese manga. I found myself not only emotionally invested in the narratives but increasingly drawn to the language and culture behind them. That growing desire was further deepened by my friendship with my best friend and his wife—both Korean—as well as the many Korean students I met and got to know at my university.

From there, I began watching K-dramas, Korean reality and

variety shows, and slowly, re-entered the world of K-pop—this time through groups like BTS, Stray Kids, BLACKPINK, ASTRO, and SHINee. And as it often happens on YouTube: One search led to another, and soon I found myself spiraling down the K-pop rabbit hole.

The deeper I went, the more fascinated I became with K-pop as an industry—particularly by its many contradictions.

K-pop is beautiful.

But it's also brutal.

A world full of dazzling light… but where, if you look closer, many dark and tragic shadows linger offstage.

Through my personal research—documentaries, interviews, news articles, and conversations with Korean friends, students, and colleagues—I began to feel that there was a story here, waiting to be told.

A tale that lives at the intersection of adoration and isolation, of fame and identity, of grief and longing.

That story became the two parts of *Death of an Idol*.

And because the setting and the industry I'm exploring is so rich, layered, and emotionally intricate, I knew from the start that the stories I wanted to capture couldn't be confined to a single book without compromising on its depth and quality.

Together, *Death of an Idol* Book 1 and the upcoming Book 2 explore not just the mystery at the heart of the story, but the deeper psychological and emotional threads running beneath it.

This story touches on difficult themes and topics relating to violence, murder, abuse, self-harm and obsession. These are not easy subjects. But fiction gives us space to explore what's painful and often unspoken. It allows us to ask uncomfortable questions and to stretch our empathy beyond the boundaries of our own experience.

This is a book about idols.

Also about those who love them.

The ones who lose them.

And the ones who can't let go…

Novel Playlist

Music is central to the world of this story—and to the characters who live in it.

As such, *Death of an Idol* is an immersive, multisensory reading experience—one that blends music with narrative to deepen emotion and atmosphere.

Throughout the book, you'll find suggested soundtracks woven into the story and tied to specific scenes. Some are K-pop numbers; others are cinematic or ambient pieces that shaped the rhythm of my writing.

This is an experimental style of storytelling—one you may not have encountered before, and one that may not be for everyone.

If it's not for you, feel free to skip the cues.

The story stands on its own.

But if you're someone who, like me, feels deeply through music—especially if you're a K-pop fan or a music lover— these tracks might draw you deeper into the characters' inner worlds.

Below is a playlist of the songs that echoed in my ears and inspired me as I wrote *Death of an Idol,* Book 1. These pieces helped shape the emotional and psychological landscape of the novel. I encourage you to revisit the story with these melodies in your ears—may the music guide you and be your companion as you read.

Book 1 Playlist

"Moonlight Sonata" — Ludwig van Beethoven, *Prologue*

"Red Lights" — Bang Chan and Hyunjin (Stray Kids), *Chapter 5*

"Where Am I" — Cha Eunwoo, *Chapter 6*

"Love and War" — Fleurie, *Chapter 7*

"From the Beginning till Now" — Ryu, *Chapter 12*

"Once Upon a Dream"—Lana Del Rey, *Epilogue*

Prologue

[Suggested soundtrack: *Beethoven's "Moonlight Sonata."*]

IT WAS A BEAUTIFUL DAY.

The sun shimmered high over the windswept cliffs of Seopjikoji, a remote stretch along Jeju Island's eastern coast.

The beach was quiet. The only sounds audible were the waves rhythmically washing up on the shoreline as if humming a lullaby.

The ocean glittered under the sunlight, unfurling like the endless train of a bridal gown, varying in blueish-green shades of teal and turquoise near the shoreline then gradually morphing into a magnificent cobalt—eventually merging into sapphire blue in the distance.

If there was heaven on earth, it would be here.

She looked up at the sky, her hands outstretched, as the waves swayed back and forth caressing the outline of her petite frame. Her flawless honey complexion glowed as the rays of the sun danced on her beautifully sculpted face while illuminating her long slender neck and bare shoulders.

A gentle breeze occasionally lifted the burgundy curls partially covering her face. The mild breeze wafted in the aroma of the sea.

As she inhaled the scent of ocean brine, her mind flashed back to their first trip to Hawaii as a couple. That day as

1

they had cuddled together on a shared towel on the beach on Maui, their bodies intertwined, kissing while staring into the beautiful sunset, she had made him promise. Promise that if they ever got married they would travel to a beach destination for their honeymoon.

From the corner of her eye, she noticed the flash of light sparkling off the pink diamond solitaire on her finger, complemented by her immaculately manicured nails in her favorite shade of rose pink.

Most girls dream of their wedding. The perfect bridal dress, the wedding venue, the company of family and friends, the elaborate vows and rituals—not her. With a heart battered and broken by one failed relationship after another since high school, she was tired of the cycle of picking up the pieces of her shattered heart and piecing it back together.

"No more," she had promised herself when her three-year-long engagement with her ex, had ended with him abandoning her at the altar. Leaving her to live her worst nightmare, alone and humiliated in front of all their family, friends, and loved ones.

It was that day while sobbing on her mother's lap, just as she had done since childhood, that she came to a realization. Even as her family and friends banded around her unleashing curses, threats, and insults on her ex while soothing her, she realized that the elaborate ceremony in Napa valley, the lavish bridal dress, the heart-shaped Tiffany's ring she had carefully picked, the three-tiered wedding cake, bridal attendants, parade-like processions—they all meant *nothing*.

What mattered to her most was to simply be married 'till death do us part' to the man she loved.

As she looked up, she could see the majestic fifty-foot cliff above her. It was hard to imagine that just a few minutes back, she was at the top of the cliff posing in front of the breathtaking scenery.

And now she was lying at the bottom of that cliff in a pool of ever-expanding blood.

As her vision blurred, she saw a figure at the top of the cliff that she recognized.

The same person who'd smiled as they took her phone. Who had coaxed her to the edge. Who'd told her to hold still, turn around, just one more shot.

Who had waited… and shoved.

The figure was looking directly down at her.

Watching her.

Like a vulture circling its prey.

Waiting for it to die.

They stood at the edge of the cliff as they sifted through her phone—methodically erasing photos and messages—wiping it clean.

They now approached her slowly, a gentle smile playing on their lips.

She wanted to call for help.

But she knew it was too late.

Just as she knew, that this person advancing toward her, whom she had trusted, would not save her.

The figure loomed above her. Then lowered into a crouch, close enough for her to feel their warm breath as they leaned in.

"Biane…" they whispered—*Sorry*—like a prayer, as if that one word could absolve them, could undo the irreversible.

Then with cold precision a gloved hand reached for her fingers. She felt the tug as the ring slipped away.

3

They then placed her phone—now wiped clean—neatly beside her.

From where she lay she could hazily see her screen a few feet away. A happy picture of her laughing, enveloped in the arms of the man she loved.

Her heart ached seeing his face.

The future they had once imagined—every fragile dream, every tender plan—was fading away. Their house with the red door. The fall wedding they had been planning beneath a canopy of red and gold leaves, reading their handwritten vows. Their child with her dimple and his eyes. The echo of their small feet pattering down a hallway.

She tried extending her fingers to grab the phone but couldn't reach it.

As her consciousness gradually started to drift, she watched the figure depart, leaving her with only one final thought.

Why?

Chapter 1

DARKNESS BLURRED THE EDGES of Park Tae-joon's vision.

The world around him was indistinct. A dull gray non-descript hotel room.

A sterile suite, a king size bed with blackout curtains drawn shut, the muffled hum of city traffic seeping through.

His phone buzzed against the nightstand, the screen lighting up the darkness. He blinked, disoriented.

3:00 AM.

He didn't know what day it was.

It didn't seem to matter.

He reached for the phone. The name flashing on the screen made his breath catch.

Mino.

"Hyung?" The hesitation in his voice clung to that word—Korean for *older brother.*

It was a voice he recognized—but not like this.

Raw. Shaken. Unsteady.

Tae's brow knit in concern.

"Mino? Wae geurae?"

(Mino? What's wrong?)

Silence stretched for a beat too long.

Then, his voice came through—low, shaky.

"*H-hyung... na... na eotteokhae?*"

(Hyung... I... I don't know what to do.)

"*Eonje wa? Jebal…*"

(When are you coming back? Please…)

Tae sat up in bed, his pulse quickening.

He hadn't heard from Mino in weeks—not since the reunion anniversary stream they'd all half-heartedly agreed to participate in.

"I'm working on a shoot here in Tokyo—will be back in Seoul by the end of the week."

Another pause.

Then a whisper:

"*Geuttaen neomu neujeulji molla.*"

(It might be too late by then.)

Tae's skin prickled. A cold sensation began spreading through his chest, heavier with each breath.

"Too late? Mino-ya… what are you talking about? What's going on?"

"*Hyung, na—*" Mino's voice cracked. "*Naneun mujaweo.*"

(Hyung, I— I'm scared.)

"*Jinjja... hal mal isseo.*"

(There's something I really need to tell you.)

Tae's fingers tightened around the phone.

"*Mu-wo-ya? Malhae bwa.*"

("What is it? Tell me.")

No answer, just heaving breathing.

There was a sound on the other end—a beep followed by a click.

And then—

what sounded like a low whistle.

6

A slow, melodic tune.

Vaguely familiar—but just out of reach.

It was faint, barely audible over the crackle of static.

Mino's breathing quickened.

"*Na... jigeum mot malhae.*"

(I... I can't talk now.)

Static.

Heavy breathing.

"*Mino-ya? Yeoboseyo? Mino-ya?*"

("Mino? Hello? Mino?")

The line cut.

Tae bolted upright in bed, chest heaving.

Sweat clung to his skin, and the sheets were tangled around his legs. He glanced at the digital clock on the nightstand.

3:00 AM.

Just a dream, he told himself.

A dream of what happened that day—five years back.

He opened his phone gallery and tapped into his favorites, landing on a picture he hadn't been able to delete or replace in years.

The five of them, side by side, arms slung around each other, laughing in a moment that felt impossibly distant now.

The boys of Orion—Tae, Duri, Mino, Jaeho and Rian.

So young, hopeful... so alive.

His eyes found Mino.

Mino had always stood out, even in the spotlight. A delicate, almost ethereal beauty—with doe-like eyes framed by thick lashes, light pink hair, a soft jawline that barely hinted at his youth. His smile was small but radiant.

He had been the soul of the group, a genius with lyrics, and vocals that could shatter hearts. All their hit numbers were

7

written by him. Sensitive, empathetic, and endlessly talented. He was only twenty-five when—

A lump formed in his throat so suddenly, he couldn't swallow.

He curled his back slightly, wrapping his arms around his knees, his breath catching in his throat. The guilt that had dulled to a constant hum over the years now surged like fresh blood from an old wound.

I should have called back. I should have gotten on a flight. I should have known that "I'm afraid" meant something more than a moment of anxiety.

But he had been too caught up in his work, too focused on his commitments, too confident that Mino would be fine. That everything would blow over.

But it hadn't.

Tae had reported everything to the police after Mino's death. He told them about the call—the fear in Mino's voice, the beep followed by the click, and that strange whistle in the background.

He was convinced it wasn't some random noise.

Someone had been there with him.

But the police hadn't listened. They'd dismissed it as emotional distress. There were no signs of forced entry. No clear evidence of a second person. Only one officer had taken him seriously—a junior detective, Yoon Hana.

She had looked him in the eye, listened without interrupting. She had believed him.

But even she had limits. The pressure from above was swift. There was only so much a junior officer could do. The executives at Glimmer were also keen to suppress any controversy.

Within days, the case was closed. From Seoul to New York, the headlines splashed across digital screens around the globe.

```
IDOL MINO OF ORION FOUND DEAD
27 May 2019
Seoul, South Korea

The South Korean entertainment industry is mourning
the sudden death of Mino (real name: Lee Min-oh),
the 21-year-old singer-songwriter and beloved member
of popular idol group Orion. Gangnam police
confirmed early this morning that Mino was found
unresponsive outside his residence in Seoul, having
reportedly fallen from the balcony of his 18th-floor
apartment in the early hours of the morning.

Emergency responders arrived at the scene shortly
after 5:20 AM KST, following reports from a neighbor
who heard a loud crash and notified authorities.
Mino was pronounced dead at the scene.

"There were no indications of foul play," said Chief
Inspector Yoon Sang-min of the Gangnam District
Police.

Mino debuted in 2017 as the lead vocalist and
lyricist of Orion, under Glimmer Entertainment. The
group rose to meteoric fame with hits like Starlight
and Supernova, earning a devoted Korean and
international fanbase and critical acclaim for their
artistic and introspective lyrics, many of which
were penned by Mino himself.

He was widely regarded as the "soul" of the group,
known for his haunting vocal range and poetic
songwriting.
```

```
In an official statement released earlier today,
Glimmer Entertainment said:

"We are heartbroken by the passing of our artist and
friend. Mino was a treasured part of our family. His
creativity, sensitivity, and kindness touched
everyone who worked with him. We ask for privacy and
compassion during this difficult time as we grieve
this profound loss."
```

Within a few hours of the news, candlelight vigils were organized outside the agency's headquarters. Thousands gathered, holding photos, playing Orion's music from their phones. Messages written on sticky notes covered entire walls—words of love, grief, disbelief.

Fans left letters, bracelets, plush toys, and rows of white chrysanthemums outside the dorm building where he had lived. Bouquets arrived from all over the world. The news played footage of crowds sobbing in the rain, the candle flames shivering in the wind.

And yet, only a few weeks later, it was as though the country had taken a collective breath... and exhaled him.

The vigils disappeared.

The hashtags faded.

Life went on.

But Tae could not move on.

The world's ability to forget Mino so easily felt cruel. The ease with which everyone moved on left him hollow. He wrapped up his commitments, completed the shoot of his final project *Sakura Nights*—a quiet art-house film in Tokyo—and quit the industry. He didn't even attend the film's premiere at Cannes, hadn't been back to Korea since then.

For a moment, all Tae could hear was the thundering of his heart and the echo of Mino's voice from that night in his ears.

"Hyung, naneun mujaweo."

(Hyung, I'm scared.)

"Biane, Mino-ya…" he murmured, eyes lifting, the apology barely audible in the silence.

He reached for his phone with slightly trembling hands, needing to anchor himself. He closed his eyes and sat in the dark, phone clenched tight.

The air in the room felt stale and heavy. Claustrophobic.

Tae rose and headed to the bathroom. Steam ghosted over the mirror as heat from the shower rose. He stripped down and stepped into the water, letting it cascade over him like rain, hoping it would wash away his anxiety.

At six-foot-one, Tae's body was lean but strong—long limbs, strong lines. His shoulders were broad and commanding, tapering down into a narrow waist, his frame balanced in perfect proportion. It was as if a sculptor had lovingly shaped him by hand—like some forgotten god molded from porcelain and brought to life.

Water traced along the lines of his collarbone, gliding down his chest and over the contours of his abdomen, catching for a moment in the shallow dip just above his hipbones, before sliding lower. His hair clung to his forehead, dark and wet, drawing attention to his face.

A face that had been appraised and analyzed by millions—across Korea and beyond. Deemed perfectly symmetrical by cameras, fans, and algorithms alike: a straight, high-bridged nose; full lips that curled into a naturally soft smile; smooth, luminous skin; and a defined jawline that angled gracefully into a chin.

But it was his eyes that held you.

Amber-hazel, vivid and startling like embers catching light. They burned with warmth and intensity. In certain angles and lighting, they glowed gold. Eyes like that didn't just look at you, they pulled you in—like fire.

Mesmerizing, untouchable, threatening to consume you.

It was no wonder that during his days as an idol, fans would gather in the thousands just for a glimpse of "Adonis" or "Face Prodigy"—as he was popularly referred to in Korea. Brands had scrambled to have him front their campaigns. Over time, the label had stopped being just a nickname.

It became his identity.

And while he'd been grateful for the admiration, for the endless attention—he had always longed for something more enduring. For his talent, his skills, and his work to be what people remembered.

Not just his face.

It had taken him years to build his reputation as a dependable and versatile actor, starting with limited screen time side roles, before being offered projects as the lead.

And his efforts had eventually started to pay off, as critics who had previously only commented on the beauty of his face, started to move beyond and appreciate how his face could convey a range of emotions with precision—appearing soulful, melancholic, or piercing depending on the scene.

But then, just as his career was gaining traction, he walked away.

These days almost no one recognized him.

And for that, he was grateful.

Tae dried off, tugged on a hoodie and sweats, then padded barefoot across the room stepping out onto the narrow balcony of his downtown Pittsburgh apartment.

The city stretched out below him: hushed under the soft glaze of night, save the occasional hum of passing cars or the distant barking of a restless dog.

Tae leaned against the balcony, the wind cool against his face.

The streetlights flickered red over wet pavement. There was something about the lights—their steady, pulsing glow—that unlocked a door in his memory.

It brought him back.

To the stage.

To that night.

Back in Seoul. Back when they were still five.

Their final concert as Orion.

The moment was burned into him.

The arena had gone dark. A brief hush—a collective inhale from the crowd—tens of thousands holding their breath as one.

Then—

A blast of blinding white light tore through the darkness, and the crowd erupted.

An explosion. A sound like thunder, like the birth of stars.

The roar of Stardust, what their fans called themselves, rose like a tidal wave—deafening, euphoric.

Glow sticks swayed like waves in the dark, moving in unison, like fireflies in perfect formation. A galaxy of movement, hypnotic, endless—a living ocean of devotion.

Their fans filled every seat, every stairwell, every standing zone. They screamed their names, their voices colliding into a single feverish chant.

They had camped for days, many arriving from overseas—Japan, the U.S., Malaysia, Hong Kong—braving sleepless nights, hunger, cold. Just to be there.

The five of them stood together—Orion—side by side, shoulder to shoulder. Arms linked. Faces wet with sweat and emotion.

Tae remembered the costumes they had worn that night: sapphire velvet jackets tailored to their frames, silver embroidery shaped like constellations stitched across the sleeves and lapels. Underneath, layered black mesh and leather, sprinkled with glitter, designed to catch light with every turn.

A moving constellation.

Mino's was different. His jacket had a winged motif—embroidered with sweeping silver wings. He had insisted on it, saying he wanted to "fly tonight."

The beat dropped.

The crowd went wild.

And they danced.

Every movement hit hard, sharp, liquid-smooth. Spins and drops. Footwork synchronized to the millisecond. Arms slicing air. Bodies arching, folding, striking poses in perfect time.

The heat on stage was searing—lights blazing from every angle, the floor beneath them vibrating with bass.

Tae remembered the ache in his body from hours of rehearsals, the tightness of his outfit clinging to him like a second skin, the earpiece crackling faintly with their manager's voice, reminding them to smile.

But the adrenaline kept them going.

He could still hear them—chanting, crying, singing. Their

fans knew every lyric. Every choreographed cue.

Then came the bridge.

The stage dimmed to deep red. Strobes pulsed like lightning through fog.

Mino stepped forward, his solo cutting through the air like silk—his voice aching, sublime.

Tae, just a step behind him, remembered that moment with startling clarity: Mino's eyes closed, his mouth curving into the softest smile. He looked lit from within.

That was the last time Tae would see him like that—not framed in photographs or frozen beneath headlines. But real.

Unbelievably radiant. Unbearably alive.

Mino turned slightly, catching Tae's eye mid-breath. Just for a second. His face grinning wide, flushed and breathless, eyes shining like a boy who still couldn't believe this was real. He lifted his hand in the air and flashed a finger heart, twirling with a playful spin before winking at the crowd, who erupted in screams.

Then the final chorus crashed in.

Lights flared gold.

Confetti exploded from the rafters.

The bass throbbed beneath their feet.

Tae felt it in his chest like a second heartbeat.

The audience's hands moved like waves in time with the song. Phones glowed. Voices merged. The sound was deafening and tender all at once. The five of them raised their arms, hands clasped, heads bowed toward the crowd.

And for one breathless moment—they weren't idols.

They weren't even human.

They were gods—immortal, untouchable, divine.

Now, the city was quiet beneath him.

Just the hush of late-night traffic and the blare of far-off sirens.

He reached into his hoodie, fingers hoping to brush against the familiar edge of a crumpled pack of cigarettes.

The impulse was still there. But he paused.

Sonia hated it when he smoked. It had been one of the first things she requested him to do when they started dating. And he had kept up his commitment for the last four years.

He turned to his nicotine gum, chewing it slowly, trying to smother the urge. He focused on his phone, scrolling through nothing in particular—anything to keep himself distracted.

But as the screen's glow reflected off his face, a strange sensation began to creep in. A familiar prickle along the back of his neck.

He hadn't felt it in years, not since his days in the spotlight. The feeling of being watched.

Then—

Click.

The faint but unmistakable sound of a camera shutter.

He looked around sharply. The shadows across the street shifted, but he couldn't see anyone. Darkness pooled between the alleyways, windows dimly lit, no movement.

His chest tightened.

Who would take a picture of him here?

No one knew where he lived apart from Sonia.

But clearly someone had found him.

He scanned the street below, heart thudding.

No footsteps. No flash. Nothing.

Just that sound.

Click.

And suddenly, a chill crept in.

16

Tae felt the weight of unseen eyes...
of a past that refused to stay buried.

Chapter 2

THE ROOM WAS BARELY the size of a parking space. The low ceiling trapped the smell of old kimchi, damp laundry, and something sour that never went away.

Carboard boxes lined the walls of the room, spilling clothes on the floor. The floor was cold, no matter the season. In the summer, heat stuck to their backs. In winters, their toes turned numb even under three layers of covers.

There was no bed. Just a pile of thin, itchy blankets.

In the far corner of the room, a child sat quietly, knees pulled beneath the hem of a pink polka dot dress, the fabric faded and fraying along the seams.

Her long black hair was held back by a faded Minnie Mouse headband tilted slightly askew. It crowned an angelic face: ivory-pale with beautiful almond-shaped brown eyes framed by lashes so long they almost touched her cheeks.

She looked like a delicate china doll left forgotten on a shelf.

The little girl hadn't eaten all day, but her face gave nothing away. Hunger had become a familiar ache—something to ignore, something to endure.

In the dead stillness of the room, the TV in the corner was the only thing that felt alive. It flashed, glowed, made noise. Unlike the child—motionless, mute—who never made a sound, never cried.

Crying made noise. Noise drew attention. And in this house, attention could be dangerous.

The child had learned that early—lessons etched into the skin through bruises along her small ribs and faint crescent-shaped scars near the collarbone where fingernails had once sunk in.

The first time a cry had slipped out was when Abeoji—her father—had thrown away her favorite doll. It had ended with the back of her head slamming into the floor.

That day, she learned: crying only brought more pain.

So, tears became dangerous. And sobs—even the smallest ones—had to be swallowed before they ever reached the surface. After that, silence became instinct.

Beyond the sliding door, an argument had started again.

"I'm done. I can't live like this anymore. They came *again* today. How are we going to pay them?"

"You think I don't know that? You think I'm not trying? I said I'll handle it!"

"Handle it… how?" she asked, her feeble voice, shaking now. "We have *nothing*. No money. No food. What about Nari? She's hasn't eaten all day."

"I keep telling you to shut up and stop with that bullshit about her already—I've had enough!"

"Why? She is your daughter too. But you don't give a damn about her. But I do. I'm her mom. She's all I've got! She—"

Then came a loud crash—something shattered, maybe a dish

or a glass—followed by the unmistakable sound of a slap.

A moment of stunned silence.

"I'm sorry," he said quietly, almost a whisper.

"Why do you always push me like this? Why do you keep saying things you know will set me off?" he said, trying to keep his voice steady.

Then her muffled cry, followed by the sound of the front door being slammed a few seconds later.

The little girl squeezed her eyes shut and waited.

Always waited. Listening closely. Counting backward from ten in her head:

"Yeol... ahop... yeodeol... ilgop..."

(Ten... night... eight... seven...)

By the time she reached *hana*, silence descended over the apartment. No more shouting.

Gentle footsteps approached.

Then, a soft familiar voice

"Nari-ya... gwaenchanha. Ije gwaenchanha."

(Nari... it's okay. It's okay now.)

Eomma, she thought.

The tension in her tiny shoulders began to ease.

Eomma came in quietly, careful not to make the floorboards creak as if the wood might betray her, then gently lowered herself to the floor.

Nari looked up. Eomma's cheek was already swelling, a dark plum shade blooming beneath her eye. A cut ran along the side of her lip, faint but fresh.

One of the buttons on Eomma's favorite red cardigan was missing. And her wrist—barely visible beneath her stretched sleeve—was mottled black and blue from the week before, like ink seeping into the skin.

When she reached for the remote, her hand trembled slightly. But her voice was light. Almost cheerful.

"Let's watch our favorite show?" she said while brushing a strand of Nari's long hair behind her ear like nothing had happened.

Nari nodded and put up a small smile for Eomma, curling up beside her and gently touching her bruised arm.

Eomma smiled in that moment, soft and fragile, her lips trembling, tears brimming in her eyes. But before they could fall, she quickly turned her face toward the TV—refusing to let her child see her come undone.

She turned the volume up.

The TV flared into color, filling the dark room with sudden warmth. The theme song played, soft and chipper.

It was *Uri Jib Mujigae*—Rainbow Family—one of Korea's most beloved family sitcoms. For thirty minutes every evening, it made people believe in perfect homes and peaceful dinners. It offered a picture of a world where families loved each other, kindness and goodness always won, and no one ever raised their voice in anger.

The show's jingle began as a cartoon rainbow arched across the screen and the Lee family danced in front of their beautiful home:

Urineun mujigae gajok-ieyo!
  (We are the Rainbow Family!)

Appaneun useum, eommaneun haetsal,
  (Daddy brings the laughter, Mommy brings the sunshine)

21

Aideureun byeolcheoreom banjjag-yeoyo.
(And the kids shine like little stars)

Da hamkke sonjapgo noraehaeyo—haengbog-i uri
jip!
*(Let's all hold hands and sing—Happiness lives in our
home!)*

On-screen, the Lee family beamed: a handsome Appa (father)
in a sweater vest, a beautiful Eomma (mother) in an apron
with a floral print, and their loving adeul (son), Jiho, dressed
in a spotless school uniform—all three holding hands as they
bowed to the audience, welcoming them into their home.

Nari stared at Jiho.

The child actor playing the character had the look of
someone born to be adored. His skin was smooth and
unblemished. His shiny black hair was always neatly parted,
perfectly combed, not a strand out of place. His eyes were large
and kind. Even his ears looked delicate, like they belonged on
a boy in a picture book.

And he was always smiling.

But it was not just his looks that enthralled Nari, Jiho was
the "perfect son" in every way. He brought his mom a glass of
water when she coughed. He held his friend's backpack as she
tied her shoes. He stood up to bullies in class when they made
fun of the new student. He made his dad proud by coming in
first in both school and sports.

Even when he was scolded by his parents, he bowed, apolo-
gized sweetly, and hugged them both like they were the most
precious people in the world.

The character and portrayal struck such a chord with

viewers that Jiho became known across the country as "Korea's son."

To Nari, Jiho's world didn't feel like fiction.

It felt real... and beautiful—unlike her own.

In Lee Jiho's family everyone was happy. There were no broken dishes, no yelling behind thin walls. Just hugs, warm dinners, and plenty of love.

As the show played, Eomma smiled, her fingers moving gently through Nari's hair gathering one section at a time and weaving them into pigtails—sealing their quiet, daily ritual.

"Jiho is such a good boy. . ." she murmured. "You should grow up and marry someone *just* like him."

As the episode came to an end, the Lee family laughed together on the couch—Jiho leaning into his mother's side, the father reaching over to tousle his hair as they all smiled at the camera.

The screen faded into a commercial, then cut to black as Eomma rose and left to prepare dinner.

But Nari stayed still, eyes transfixed on the screen.

For a moment, it felt like something inside her was pulling, reaching. Like if one could just lean forward far enough, they could slip through the glass. Onto that couch. Into that family.

To laugh with them.

To be welcomed.

To be held.

To be loved.

Nari didn't speak. Didn't move. But something inside her shifted that day—a quiet snap, like a key turning into a lock.

A longing. A need.

I want to be with Jiho. I want be part of his family.

The good boy. The perfect boy.

The boy who never caused pain.
The boy whose family smiled at him.
The boy who was loved.

Chapter 3

THE ALARM HAD GONE off an hour ago.
Tae had silenced it without thinking.
When he finally woke, it was past eight.

He checked his phone.

No new messages.

He stared at the ceiling, heart ticking louder with each second.

Eventually he forced himself out of bed and into the small bathroom.

The space was cramped and dated—peeling, discolored tiles; a medicine cabinet that refused to stay shut. In winter, air seeped through the poorly insulated window above the tub, and the faucet squeaked each time he turned it on.

It wasn't much, but on a PhD stipend, this was the best he could afford—and only a fifteen-minute walk from the university.

Good enough for him.

The cold water slapped his face, jarring him awake. He brushed his teeth methodically; each stroke was deliberate—trying to ground himself in routine.

Routine kept him sane.

This was his life now: a fourth-year PhD student at the elite

Carriston University in downtown Pittsburgh.

It was as far as one could get from the glitz and glamour of his former idol life.

He examined his reflection. He didn't like looking in the mirror. He avoided it most mornings, glancing only long enough to shave.

With a practiced motion, he pulled on his hoodie, tucked his hair beneath a black cap, and slid the thick black-rimmed glasses into place. His camouflage—his daily armor—was complete.

No one would believe that Park Taejoon, the former idol, the face of Orion, walked among them.

As he stepped out of the bathroom, his cat, a calico Maine coon, brushed against his legs, meowing in greeting; her fluffy tail curling up like a question mark in the air.

"*Annyeong*, Lola-ya," Tae murmured, bending to scoop food into her dish.

(Hello, Lola)

The apartment was clean, minimal.

Books stacked in neat towers beside a desk, one wall plastered with academic papers and notes. A lone window let in a trickle of gray morning light.

He padded over to the kitchenette, opened the fridge, and pulled out a Tupperware with two slices of leftover pepperoni pizza. After heating them in the microwave, he ate the slices standing up, alternating bites with sips of Diet Coke.

In his idol trainee days, pizza was a forbidden luxury—practically contraband. A single slice would earn him an extra hour on the treadmill; and their manager was known to snatch a slice right out of their hands mid-bite. Back then, it was all measured calories, lean proteins, and supervised meals.

26

Now, he could eat whatever he wanted. It was freedom in the smallest, most mundane form. It may have seemed trivial to most—a small, everyday choice—but to him, it was monumental.

By 9:00, he was walking into the glass-paneled atrium of Carriston's Stranton School of Business. The building was sleek and modern, with clean lines, open spaces, and an airy design that gave it the feeling of possibility. Sunlight streamed through the skylights above, casting reflections on the polished floors.

He took the elevator to the fourth floor. His office was a small open shared space for PhD students. Three desks sat perpendicular to each other, the writable glass boards filled with econometric models and supply chain diagrams.

Roger looked up as Tae entered.

"Yo, Tae! Damn, haven't seen you in a while. You alive?"

"Barely," Tae muttered, offering a thin smile.

"Thesis hell?"

"That… and insomnia."

"You know what you need—chocolate chip pancakes," Roger declared. "With banana and Nutella. Mmm… that always gives me happy dreams."

Tae chuckled.

Tara, the other PhD student from Japan sharing their space, walked in behind him, quiet as always. Her round glasses slid a little down her nose as she offered Tae a polite smile.

"Morning," she mumbled, not meeting his gaze.

"Morning, Tara," he replied.

She hesitated, then added softly, "You look tired today. Everything okay?"

Tae nodded. "I will be, once I get through this thesis

meeting."

Tara and Roger nodded in quiet understanding, the latter giving him a thumbs up for luck as he made his way to his advisor's office on the fifth floor.

Dr. Ruby Roy sat in her chair, surrounded by an eclectic collection of books—everything from *Game Theory and Strategic Decision-Making* to *Murder on the Orient Express* by Agatha Christie. A well-worn copy of *The Art of War* sat beside an electronic Maneki-neko, the iconic beckoning cat said to bring good fortune.

She looked up from her computer as he knocked.

"Come in!" she said, gesturing at him to take a seat.

As Tae sat down, she narrowed her eyes while looking at his face. "One of those all-nighters again?"

"Something like that," he said smiling faintly.

"*Gwenchana, gwenchana… fighting!*" she said enthusiastically, raising a fist—a gesture of encouragement that meant, "It's okay. You've got this."

Tae laughed under his breath. "That was pretty good."

"Yeah? Thanks! I've been practicing!" she said with a grin, leaning forward as she flipped through the pages of his thesis draft, her pen tapping lightly on the edge of her desk.

Tae sat quietly, watching her face, awaiting her verdict with a patience that masked his nerves.

The truth was, jumping from idol life into academia had been jarring. Sure, he'd always been good at school—graduating top of his class with a business degree from Seoul National University, one of Korea's best.

But that didn't make the transition any easier.

Restarting his education, especially an advanced degree like a PhD, after years out of the game meant starting from the bottom. In this new world, his fame and past accolades carried no value.

He'd had to start fresh, rebuild from the ground up, and prove himself all over again.

"Your framework for the decision-making model is solid," Ruby finally said, "but I think your methodology needs a little tightening."

"Especially in that second case study," she continued, "you're relying heavily on qualitative interviews, but the sample size is small and lacks industry variation. Maybe try diversifying your data pool with a few international comparisons."

Tae nodded, jotting down her comments.

"Sure, I can expand on that. Maybe pull in some firms from Germany or Japan."

"Also… your data analysis in section four is too descriptive. Need to tie it back to your hypotheses—make it tighter."

"Got it. I can tweak that."

She gave him a long, appraising look.

"Honestly, you're making good progress. I think you can submit your draft to the committee next month."

Tae hesitated.

Ruby didn't miss it.

She folded her arms, tone soft but probing.

"Okay, real talk… I've known you for a while now. I don't think this is just about the research. It's something else… right?"

He looked up, startled.

"You could have graduated last year," she said, her tone matter-of-fact. "Easily!"

"You're one of my strongest students, but it feels like you're stalling—almost as if you don't want to leave this place."

29

He didn't answer immediately.

"That obvious?" he asked quietly.

"Kind of," she said gently.

"Look, I get it—this place feels safe. And you're doing great work. But sometimes, we bury ourselves in work because we don't want to deal with what's next."

He kept his head down.

"Tae, you're brilliant. That's never been the question," she continued. "Whether it's an R1 placement in the U.S. or something back in Korea, you'll have options—and you'll do great. You are ready."

Tae nodded slowly, offering a small, grateful smile.

He knew his supervisor was right.

Every time the thought of graduation loomed, so did the anxiety. Graduating meant facing the world. Facing everything he had locked away. Out there, he was still Park Tae-Joon—the ex-idol, the star who had disappeared.

Was he ready to be found again?

This was his sanctuary. Here, he was just another nobody in a hoodie and jeans.

As he returned to the office, Roger greeted him with a grin.

"So… I watched *Revenge Sonata* on Netflix last night. That new K-drama?"

"Uh-huh," Tae mumbled, eyes on his thesis draft.

"It's nuts. Wife cheats on husband, then sits him down to say she wants a divorce. He's all, 'Sure, honey,' and even cooks her favorite meal like everything's cool."

"And then guess what?" Roger paused dramatically.

"BAM—she's dead!" he exclaimed. "And the husband pins it all on the lover. Wife dead, lover boy in jail. Boom! Revenge complete. Karma deluxe edition."

Tae smirked. "Sounds wholesome."

"But seriously, why is everyone in Korean dramas always out for revenge? What happened to chill love stories?"

"Revenge is our national hobby," Tae quipped, giving him a wink.

"Remind me not to cross you guys!" Roger said, raising his hands in mock surrender.

Tae laughed.

"By the way, the lead guy in that show," Roger went on, oblivious to Tae's fading interest. "He's actually really good... Jae something? Jae Shim? Or was it Kim?"

He tapped quickly on his keyboard, then turned his laptop around.

"Here—Jaeho Kim. That's him."

Kim Jaeho.

The name hit Tae like a cold wind.

He immediately recalled the eager, fresh-faced trainee who was just starting out—a boy with relentless energy and stars in his eyes.

Jaeho had followed him everywhere, a constant presence in Tae's peripheral vision. At first, Tae had found him annoying— always hovering, always asking questions. It wasn't until his manager mentioned in passing—"You know, that kid really looks up to you,"—that Tae realized the depth of Jaeho's admiration.

He remembered a moment after a brutal dance rehearsal: He was toweling off, every muscle aching, when Jaeho had jogged up beside him, breathless, grinning from ear to ear.

"Hyung! One day I'm going to be just like you," he had said, eyes shining.

Tae had laughed then, brushing it off. But a part of him had softened that day—Jaeho's sincerity was disarming.

Over time, Tae had grown unexpectedly fond of the younger trainee. By the time Orion debuted and they became band members, that bond had only deepened.

Among the group's five members, Rian was Tae's age. Duri was older. Only Jaeho and Mino were younger—and Tae had taken to them like the little brothers he never had.

But after Mino's death, the distance between Tae and the others began to grow. Jaeho had reached out. Many times. Checking in, sending birthday messages, forwarding clips from his latest projects.

Tae had read every single one and replied to none.

Reaching out meant revisiting a version of himself he had worked hard to bury. And some ghosts were easier to miss than to face.

Now, years later, that wide-eyed trainee had transformed into the darling of Korean entertainment. As Tae looked at Jaeho's images, he realized the face he once knew hadn't changed much—only grown into the sharpness that had once been softened by youth.

Jaeho had always been beautiful, even as a rookie trainee. There was something striking about him—arresting. His face had edges, defined cheekbones, a jawline honed to perfect angles. His hair longer, often styled just slightly off-kilter, giving him the look of someone who might be too pretty for his own good—but mysterious underneath.

Like a secret only a few could touch.

The press called him a heartthrob; but his performances told a different story. He made grief look poetic and love look cruel with dark eyes that burned with something unspoken.

They didn't soften for the camera. They challenged it.

Tae remembered those eyes from years ago, in their agency's practice room, watching the choreographer's every move, memorizing every step, not missing a beat.

Back then, Jaeho was the one who stayed late into the early morning to train after everyone else had left, eyes fixed on the mirror not to admire himself—but to compete with it.

Now, those same eyes stared out from Netflix thumbnails and drama billboards, full of confidence, poise and control.

Jaeho had arrived.

He wasn't the boy standing in the wings anymore.

He *was* the show.

Tae quietly smiled. "Yeah. He's good."

The rest of the day passed in a blur.

Office hours brought the usual suspects. Three girls from his Intro to Management class waiting eagerly with highlighters and smiles too wide to be casual.

"Tae," one of them cooed, "we couldn't make it to class last week. Could you go over what we missed?"

"Sure," he replied with a soft smile.

He answered their questions patiently, knowing full well they had come just to hang out with him. But he knew how to treat them—delicately, with respect. In a way that wouldn't offend, but would still make his boundaries clear.

It was a tact, a tool, he had mastered from greeting countless female fans during his idol days. The one skill that still came in handy.

Just as they left, Roger called out, "Tae! Tara and I are grabbing lunch. You in?"

He was about to reply, when he heard his phone vibrate.

He checked it, assuming it was a text from Sonia.

But it was a message on KakaoTalk.

33

It was his mother.

"Taejoon-ah, saeng-il chukhahae."

(Taejoon, happy birthday.)

But it wasn't his birthday. Not yet.

It took him a second to realize—in Korea, it was already tomorrow.

Chapter 4

H E READ THE MESSAGE again.
"Taejoon-ah, saeng-il chukhahae."
He could almost hear it in her voice—flat, brisk, controlled—and see her face, unsmiling but trying.

His mother had never been the sentimental type. He had never once heard her say "I love you." Even when he gave his all in a performance, the highest praise she could muster was a reserved, "It's okay," or, "Not bad."

More often than not, it was followed by "But you can do better."

Praise was foreign on her tongue, affection rarer still.

Growing up, her silences cut deeper than any shouting ever could. But there was one exception—the only time he'd ever seen her lose her composure.

It was the day he told her he was leaving Korea and the entertainment industry for good.

His mother, the acting legend Park Yura—known to her fans as Y*eon-gi-ui Shin*, the "Goddess of Acting," renowned for her flawless command of emotion and her ability to summon tears or steel with surgical precision on-screen—had lost control that day.

This was the same woman who, when her husband of thirty-

35

six years died without warning, hadn't cried, hadn't flinched.

Once hailed as one of the reigning queens of Korean cinema throughout the late eighties and early nineties, she disappeared from screens one day without warning.

At twenty-seven, she gave up her career to marry Chae Hyunseok, heir to the powerful Chae Group—a vast, multi-generational chaebol empire. It was also one of Korea's oldest and most conservative chaebol families, whose legacy and reputation demanded modesty from its women and obedience from its wives.

Even though Hyunseok had fallen in love with Yura through her films, after their engagement, his family made it clear: no more films.

But Yura refused to let her ambition die. It simply changed shape—especially after the birth of her second child, Tae.

Her eldest son, Chae Minjae, was the heir apparent. And from an early age, Minjae was groomed for legacy: boardroom etiquette, overseas education, the works. Despite being his mother, Yura had no say in Minjae's upbringing.

Tae, on the other hand, was a different story.

He had Yura's beauty—clear, expressive brown eyes, effortless poise, and a face the camera adored. Realizing his star potential, Yura redirected and channeled all her energy, aspirations, and resources into him.

When her in-laws opposed, she countered that Tae wouldn't carry the burden of succession. So why not let him pursue his talent, especially given his looks and potential?

"Let him shine where Minjae would lead!" she argued.

It had taken delicate maneuvering, but Yura eventually managed to convince her father-in-law and the family to allow Tae a public life.

A life she herself had been denied.

But it came with one condition: Tae could not use the family name. They didn't want headlines associating him with corporate scandals or personal gossip.

No link between the entertainment world and the boardroom.

And so, when Tae debuted as a child-actor, he did so as Park Tae-joon—his maternal grandfather's name. He was cast in his first commercial at age three. By five, he was crying on cue in hit dramas, and by ten, he was winning awards on national television.

His mother was his manager. She had choreographed his childhood like a tightly scripted production schedule—meals, rehearsals, auditions, fan events.

So when, at twenty-three and at the height of his career, he told her he was leaving Korea for good to pursue an academic career in America and become a professor—she saw it as an act of betrayal.

"You don't walk away from this," she snapped. "Do you have any idea how many people would *kill* for the life you have? Do you realize how much I have sacrificed for you?"

"You chose this life," he had replied quietly. "I didn't."

"You're throwing everything away. Your name. Your future. If you go through with this, don't come asking me for help. I won't support you—not a *single* cent. You're on your own!"

That was the last time they spoke.

Tae texted a simple "*gomawoyo*" (thanks) in response to her message.

* * *

It was just after six when Tae got back from campus, his backpack slung over one shoulder.

He moved through the quiet lobby of his apartment building, heading straight for the mailroom tucked behind the stairwell.

A push notification had buzzed on his phone earlier—his *Luxer* box had a delivery waiting for unit 639.

The mailroom was dimly lit, the walls painted a lifeless gray, the hum of a vending machine the only sound. Tae keyed in the passcode from his phone, and the lock clicked open with a mechanical chirp.

Inside, resting neatly atop a stack of flyers, was a package—modestly sized, wrapped in delicate cream paper with a silver bow.

He paused.

His name was written in English and Hangul in soft cursive pink ink across the tag. A slow smile tugged at the corner of his mouth.

Sonia.

His chest warmed slightly as he carried it upstairs.

Back in his apartment, he set the package on the kitchen counter and peeled the paper back with care. Inside the box was a soft, cinnamon-brown teddy bear stitched with a red velvet heart, a tiny ribbon around its neck.

Tucked inside the box was a card.

He opened it.

> *Happy Birthday, Tae. This bear is so you always know you're loved. Keep it somewhere close—so I can always be with you.*

He smiled again, this time fuller.

She remembered. Of course she did.

In the past five years, Sonia had never missed his birthday.

It was her thing. And she would always find creative new ways to surprise him.

A cupcake at midnight. A secret gift under his bed. Once, she planted tiny paper cranes all over the apartment, each with a line from a poem she'd written for him. Another year, she sent him on a scavenger hunt across the city—each clue a place they'd shared, each stop a memory.

She had a way of making every day—and everything, however small—feel like it mattered. It was one of the things he'd fallen in love with: the innocent, almost childlike way, Sonia saw the world.

"Thanks, babe," he murmured, touching the card with his fingertips. He placed the bear on his nightstand, beside their engagement photo.

He missed her.

He picked up the phone and called her.

Three rings. Then her voice came through.

"Hi! This is Sonia. Leave a message!"

He smiled. Her voice was sunlight—soft, warm, lilting and always dancing on the edge of a laugh.

"Hey," he said quietly, after the tone. "It's me… I miss you. Call me back when you get this."

He hung up, his thumb lingering over the screen as he stared at her photo: a smiling face, light brown eyes sparkling full of warmth.

After his years in the entertainment industry, Tae had become cynical. He'd learned not to trust smiles that came too easily or compliments that sounded rehearsed.

Behind the glamor, he'd seen too much—manipulation

dressed as kindness, loyalty traded for clout, people who conveniently forgot you the second the lights dimmed.

But Sonia moved through the world differently.

She found wonder in things others passed by without a glance. She would smile when she saw an elderly couple holding hands or point out the way the wind tugged at a line of clothes like it was trying to dance. She loved the gentle clink of dishes in cafés, the blur of the world outside through a rainy window, the glow of bright streetlights at night.

Nothing dramatic—just moments. Small ones. But the way she noticed them made Tae look twice. Through her eyes, the world softened.

He sat on the edge of his bed, staring at the framed photo on his bedside. It was his favorite picture of her.

It was their trip to Hawaii last summer—just the two of them, barefoot and carefree, on a secluded stretch of beach as the sun dipped into the horizon after he had proposed.

She had wanted the world to know. That photo was the first she asked to post on Instagram.

He had hesitated. He hadn't been on social media in five years—not since leaving everything behind. The industry. The fandom. His family. Korea.

But in that moment, when Sonia's eyes gleamed with joy and nervous excitement, he hadn't been able to say no.

She didn't tag him, respecting his privacy. But that didn't stop people from finding him.

The post went viral overnight.

People recognized him—ex-idol, ex-actor, the missing Orion member. Comments began to roll in, including some from his Orion members:

@rianismusic: *"Chukhahae. Jal sara."*
(Congrats. Live well.)

@jaehosings: *"Ajikdo sin-gihanikka.   Haeng-bokhagil."*
(Still feels unreal. Wishing you happiness.)

Messages from Stardust, Orion's once-devoted fandom, flooded the post—some kind, some cruel.

"Wa jinjja chukhahaeyo! Neomu yeppeuseyo."
(Wow, congratulations! You're so beautiful.)

"Park Taejoon silhwanya... saraisseotne..."
(Is that really Park Tae-Joon... so he is alive...)

"Wae ireon yeojarang? Aidol sujun an matne."
(Why a woman like her? Not idol-tier at all.)

"Ttaeron idoldo saraminde... saranghaneun geot jina?"
(Sometimes idols are just human... is he in love for real?)

"Neomu dallyeotta... yeojachingu neun taekbak."
(This is so unexpected... the girlfriend is a shock.)

"Chamda... uri oppa nune an chwo."
(Sigh... our oppa doesn't have good taste.)

"Deo isang kkokjji an halge. Geunyang haeng-bokhage sarayo."
(I won't obsess anymore. Just live happily.)

"Uri Tae oppa, nuneul tteun geudaero yeppeun saramman bon geot gata."
(Our Tae oppa... looks like he just followed his heart.)

Sonia hadn't said much, but he could tell the post had gotten to her. That night, they lay tangled in bed, her head resting quietly on his chest.

"I knew you used to be famous," she murmured. "But I didn't expect a whole army of fans coming for me in the comments."

Tae groaned softly. "I told you not to post it."

"And miss my chance to cause an internet meltdown. Please!" she chuckled.

She looked up at him, a mischievous glint in her eye.

"They're just jealous because I got the 'face of Orion' and they didn't."

"Sorry ladies," she declared in a mock-serious tone, "but he's mine!"

Tae smiled, leaning down to kiss her.

Later, as she drifted off in his arms, he watched her sleep—one arm draped over him. She looked so calm, so unguarded in that moment. He had watched her like that for a long time hoping—quietly, desperately—that nothing would disturb that blissful smile, the peace she'd carved out in his arms.

Tae spent the next several hours hunched over his desk, a stack of student exams still left to grade—red ink marked the margins.

He checked the clock on his laptop.

It read 12:00.

It was now officially his birthday.

He hadn't planned anything for the day. Maybe he would order takeout and have some beer with Roger. Nothing special.

Still—he thought Sonia would call.

He glanced at his phone.

Nothing.

He tried to reassure himself—they lived in different states. She was in New York while he was in Pennsylvania. He knew this week she was meeting her editor in Manhattan. Also, it was not out of the blue for her to go quiet when deep in a manuscript, disappearing into her words.

But something felt different this time. He could sense it.

He texted her.

Miss you. Wish you were here.

His head began throbbing. He tossed the phone onto the nightstand and sank onto the bed, rubbing his temples. Maybe he just needed to shut his eyes.

He drifted into uneasy sleep.

* * *

He stood barefoot on a sun-drenched beach, the tide warm and shallow as it swept over his feet. Sonia stood a few steps ahead in a pale pink dress, her hair trailing behind her like dark smoke in the wind.

She turned to him. "I want you to remember me every time you come here."

Tae smiled. "Why would I need to remember you? We'll come together."

She said nothing.

Just smiled—soft and sad.

"The sunset is beautiful today," she whispered.

He turned to look—the sky was ablaze with color, breathtaking and surreal. Streaks of molten gold, burnt orange and coral bled into one another, fading into the faintest hint of pink blush near the horizon.

"Yeah," he said. "Really beautiful…"

When he turned back—she was gone.

The sun had vanished.

Everything was dark now.

The water no longer shimmered; it writhed and slithered like a black serpent. He saw her footprints in the sand, leading toward the sea.

"Sonia?" he called.

No response.

Panic surged through him.

He raced after the prints, heart pounding, until they disappeared at the edge of the water.

Without thinking, he ran in.

The ocean was cold now, darker than before.

Something about it felt wrong.

He dove under, calling her name, searching.

The water tugged at him like unseen hands pulling him deeper.

He gasped, choking on salt.

44

His head began to throb.

Everything was spinning.

He kicked upward, reaching for the surface—

Tae woke up breathless.

The room was still. He sat up and wiped the sweat from his forehead.

Then—

Buzz.

His phone lit up on the nightstand.

His heart surged.

Sonia?

He grabbed the phone.

But it was from Sarah—Sonia's sister

Just one line:

"Tae... it's about Sonia."

A jolt ran down his spine.

He sat up and clicked the link she'd sent beneath the text.

The page took a second too long to load.

Then the headline hit him.

"Young Woman Found Dead on Jeju Island Cliff"

He froze.

Hands trembling, he scrolled.

"The body of a woman was discovered early Monday morning by hikers at the base of the Seopjikoji cliffs, a remote and often windswept area of Jeju Island's eastern coast.

Authorities suspect the death was accidental—possibly the

> *result of a fall while attempting to take an 'insaeng' shot, a term in Korean, meaning "the best snapshot of one's life."*
>
> *Such photos, often taken from scenic or precarious locations, have become increasingly popular in recent years, with many attempting similar shots for social media.*
>
> *No signs of forced entry were found at the guesthouse where she had been staying. The victim had reportedly checked into a secluded guesthouse two days earlier under her legal name."*

Then—beneath the text—a photo.

A faded passport headshot.

Her eyes soft but direct, her smile small.

Sonia.

The phone slipped from his hands.

He crumpled to the floor.

"No... no, no—"

It wasn't real.

It couldn't be.

The room suddenly dimmed. Sound seemed to muffle. He could feel his breath shortening, the air thickening in his lungs.

He couldn't hear anything past the ringing in his ears.

He folded forward, rocking slightly as his breath came in short, sharp gasps.

As he looked up, his eyes fell on the framed engagement picture of them on his bedside mantle.

Sonia in her pale pink sundress, her hair wild from the wind.

She was laughing, head thrown back, showing off her engagement ring as he wrapped his arms around her from behind.

His vision blurred as a raw cry tore from someplace deep within him.

Deep. Broken. Feral.

The teddy bear sat still on the nightstand and watched.

Then one of its glassy eyes flickered red—just once.

A pulse of light.

* * *

A dark room lit only by monitors.

A camera feed flickered to life: Tae's bedroom

There he was—collapsed on the floor, shaking.

Someone was watching.

A chair creaked as the observer leaned in, fingers gliding over a control.

The camera zoomed in slowly.

Tae's face filled the screen—broken, flushed, soaked in sweat and tears, lips trembling.

The watcher said nothing.

Only the sound of breathing in the dark.

Heavy. Ragged. Uneven.

Chapter 5

[Suggested soundtrack: *"Red Lights" by Stray Kids. Press play when you reach: "Haah..."*]

IN A ROOM BATHED in red hues, only the screens flickered.

A giant display dominated the far wall with a live feed.

On it—Tae—asleep—his brow slightly furrowed, lips parted, face pressed gently against the pillow. He had finally surrendered to sleep, lashes still damp, tear streaks across his cheeks.

On the other side of the screen, a figure watched.

Still. Silent.

Their gaze fixed as though beholding something sacred.

The camera held still, capturing the fragile rhythm of Tae's breathing. On the other side, the watcher mirrored him— inhale, exhale—breath for breath, like a shadow.

Haah... haah... haah...

The opening notes of *Red Lights* by Stray Kids poured into the room—dark, tense, electric.

A pulsing synth rippled across the floorboards.

Bass trembled in the walls.

As the lyrics surged through the air like a fever dream, the figure rose.

Black overalls. Red boots.

A netted crimson wedding veil draped over their face, obscuring their features. Only the curve of full, painted lips—vivid and scarlet—stood out like a wound.

The beat pulsed low and steady, a fevered throb that gripped the air and refused to let go.

Then that unmistakable first drop.

As they moved, hips gyrating to the beats, one hand gloved in delicate red mesh clutched the air.

Long, lacquered nails glinted: sharp, blood-red, like talons.

There was something hypnotic in the way they moved.

This wasn't choreography.

It was instinct—raw, unfiltered, desperate.

It couldn't be learned.

It was *felt*.

A fever dream set to rhythm.

Compulsion. Possession in motion.

Surrounding them was a sea of images, thousands of them.

From floor to ceiling, every inch was covered in—

Tae.

Some glossy and high-resolution, ripped from magazine spreads and concert press kits. Others were grainy, clearly taken from afar, like long-lens surveillance.

There were images of Tae walking down a street in Pittsburgh, Tae eating in a café, Tae in a hoodie staring at a book in the library, Tae standing on his apartment balcony—each image capturing a moment never meant to be shared.

The figure watched them as they twirled; every step matching the music.

Precise. Sensual. Aching.

The photos were all pinned, taped, glued, laminated, layer upon layer, overlapping and multiplying like a mosaic of obsession.

In the midst of it all, they danced.

Like no one was watching.

Every turn, every slide, every thrust bled hunger.

If they could only dance close enough to the images, maybe, just maybe… they could slip inside and touch him.

One recent hidden camera photo showed Tae just out of the shower, body glistening, hair damp—caught in that raw, unguarded moment no one was meant to see.

The figure looked upon it almost reverently, as if bearing witness to something holy.

Beads of sweat gleamed along the curve of their jaw and down their slender neck.

As lyrics murmured through the track, their chest rose with every breath, shallow and urgent.

The gloved hand traced down their neck in a sinuous glide, drifting lower—over their collarbone, trailing down their chest—before brushing down their torso, grazing the curve of their hip.

A slow, deliberate caress, like they were savoring the idea of being held by an invisible lover only they could feel.

As they moved, the black overalls shifted just enough for a glimpse of bare skin at the waist—a narrow sliver, the delicate curve of their side visible for a fleeting moment.

The skin gleamed, flawless, luminous, like polished alabaster.

They bent backward, spine arched, as if pulled by an invisible thread.

And though the face remained veiled, the emotions radiated—desire, devotion, fury, heartbreak—all dancing on the knife's edge of madness.

Each step was an offering.

Each breath, a confession.

I love you.

I want you.

I need you.

They danced because they knew words would never be enough.

Because longing this deep had no language—only movement.

The light flickered in time with the beat, bathing the room in flashes and shades of crimson through the dark.

Black.

Then—red again.

The song reached its climax.

And as the music crescendoed,

They spun—

Arms outstretched,

Spiraling faster, tighter,

Like a storm collapsing inward.

One final, tortured twist—

And they dropped to their knees

Before the glowing main screen.

Tae's face, calm and serene.

Their gaze lowered, they knelt, pressing their forehead to the cold floor beneath the sleeping face.

As if before an altar.

A breath. A prayer. A confession.

"Neoeopsin nan sal su eopseo."

(I cannot live without you.)

Chapter 6

[Suggested soundtrack: *"Where Am I" by Cha Eunwoo. Press play at 0:27*]

TAE'S EYES OPENED, heavy and unfocused. It had been three days since he heard about Sonia.

He hadn't left the house since then—hadn't showered, hadn't eaten.

Sunlight slipped softly through the curtains, catching his face. Its warmth kissed his skin—and in that golden and gentle brightness, a memory surfaced.

"Hey, hey, close the curtains… I want to sleep a little."

"Come on, sleepyhead! It's already noon. Time to get up!" she teased, that radiant smile lighting up her face.

"Okay, but on one condition," he murmured, voice still thick with sleep.

"What?" she asked, stepping closer.

"If I get to do this—"

Without notice, he pulled her close, wrapping his arms around her as she squealed. He continued to tickle and kiss her as she broke into peals of laughter.

"Stop, stop!" she pleaded between breaths, giggling as he gently wrestled her back to her side of the bed, burying his face in the warmth of her hair.

Now, that side of the bed lay empty.

Sonia's pillow rested lonely and still.

Tae reached for it, clutching it close. He breathed in the lingering traces of her scent: it was fragile, fleeting... but still hers.

She wasn't there.

But every inch of the apartment whispered her presence: the unfinished book left open on the nightstand, her makeup and brushes scattered on the dresser, the red scarf he gifted her by the door, the tiny Christmas tree they had decorated together last December—the one she had refused to take down.

Her footprints were etched in every corner.

Everything remained... except her.

He wanted to weep—

but his eyes had run dry, with nothing left to give.

He felt like he was wading through a dense, suffocating fog, that stretched endlessly before him... no end in sight.

Over the past three days, Tae found himself questioning his existence.

The pain was overwhelming—almost unbearable at times— like sinking into an abyss of grief that threatened to swallow him whole. And part of him wanted to let it...

Lola padded over quietly, as if sensing he needed her.

Tae reached out, stroking her soft fur as he poured food into her bowl.

Feeding her were the only moments he could summon the strength to rise.

If not for Lola—he might not still be here.

But for the unbearable thought of what would happen to her if he were gone. *Who would care for her? Would they hear her cries? Would they find her? Would she wither away alone?*

That fragile thread was what had kept him tethered to life these past few days.

"*Gomawo*, Lola-ya," he whispered, burying his face in her fur. (Thank you, Lola)

She purred softly, comforting him.

Finally, he pushed back the tangled sheets and forced himself into the shower.

Standing under the hot spray, Tae struggled to piece together the questions swirling in his mind. Why had she gone to Jeju? Why didn't she tell him? Why was she there alone?

Besides him, she had no family or ties in Korea. Sonia was half American from her father's side and half Indian from her mother's. Neither of her parents had ever stepped foot in Korea.

Then there was the fact that she had told him she was in New York City, working with her editor.

Why did she lie? And why was her body found on Jeju, of all places?

These questions had been gnawing at him.

But there were no answers.

Only silence. And more questions.

Once out of the shower, Tae lay back down, eyes fixed on the photo of Sonia.

"Why were you there? Why did you go?" he asked her.

"Tell me… please. I'm going in circles. I *need* to know."

Sonia's smiling face stared back at him—now forever twenty-five. Forever beautiful.

* * *

When Tae woke up it was six.

Evening had settled over the apartment.

He had slept through most of the day again.

Slowly, almost reluctantly, he turned on his laptop. He needed to get back to his routine. Without it, he felt like he might unravel.

He scrolled through his inbox: messages from his supervisor; business research updates from academic journal subscriptions; Roger suggesting a meetup; emails from students with questions.

Then he came across something that made him pause.

He sat up straight, heart pounding as if he had seen a ghost.

An email from Sonia—dated three days ago.

The morning of his birthday.

She must have scheduled it in advance.

With trembling fingers, he opened it.

The subject read: "Surprise!!"

There were two attachments: an electronic PDF of a one-way ticket to Jeju, and an MP4 recording.

He clicked play.

There she was—

Sonia.

Alive and glowing.

Her hair dancing in the wind.

A child-like smile on her face, wide and eager.

Behind her, a windswept cliff by the sea.

"Happy birthday, baby!" she beamed, her grin bright and easy.

"I know, I know—you're probably wondering why I didn't call."

She giggled, brushing a strand of hair behind her ear.

55

"Well… I wanted to surprise you. If you forgot—this week is your birthday and… our five-year anniversary!"

She leaned in closer, excitement bubbling in her voice.

"We haven't been on a real trip since you proposed. So I thought—why not do something special?"

"Ta-da!" she said, twirling around the camera with a playful flourish, revealing the breathtaking view.

The cliff stretched wide and open, overlooking the sea—waves crashing against black jagged stones.

"You've probably guessed it already, but… I'm in Jeju!" she said.

"Surprise!"

Her smile faltered just a touch. "By the way, I'm sorry I lied to you. But you know, I can't believe you never told me Jeju was your favorite place. So… maybe we're even now?"

She laughed, trying to lighten the mood.

"Please don't be too mad, okies."

Tae's chest tightened.

It felt surreal seeing Sonia on the screen—bright, alive, talking like she was just around the corner.

For a moment, he forgot she was gone.

He longed to reach through the glass and pull her into his arms.

The lie didn't matter.

None of it did.

He just wanted her back.

He would've forgiven anything… if it meant she could come back home—just once more.

"Anyway," she continued, her voice warm, "you might've noticed the ticket I sent. I want you to come meet me. I can't wait to see you. I love you!"

She waved at the camera, then leaned in and blew him a kiss.

Tae stared at the screen, stunned—motionless—before his knees gave out and he crumpled onto the bed.

Now it made sense.

The trip. The secrecy. Why she hadn't told him.

It was supposed to be a surprise… for him.

But still—how had she known Jeju was his favorite place?

He had never mentioned it to her.

He had always avoided talk of Korea.

Had he said it in passing?   Maybe in some old Orion interview?

Even then… he still couldn't make sense of it all.

Was it really just an accident? Just an unfortunate, terrible accident?

A cold unease crept in—but before the thought could take root, his phone buzzed.

Tae stared at the message on his screen.

I'm in Pittsburgh. We need to talk.

The words were sharp, succinct.

It was from today.

And she was here.

He typed a reply.

Where are you?

The answer came within seconds.

Cafe Hestia. Fifth Ave. 20 minutes?

Tae didn't hesitate. His coat was already in his hands.

* * *

Café Hestia was the kind of place that felt displaced from time.

Its walls were lined with books in every language, the air rich with the aroma of coffee, the tables mismatched like found pieces of an old family set.

College students with their books, MacBooks and backpacks filled most of the seats.

As Tae stepped inside, he spotted her instantly—seated at a corner table by the window, her face turned toward her phone.

Seeing Tae approach, Sarah stood up, smoothing her coat, but neither moved to hug nor shake hands.

Sarah Moore stood at about five-foot-seven, taller than he remembered. Her features were a blend of sharp and soft: high cheekbones framed her oval face. Her light green eyes were lined with kohl. Her lips were pursed, as though bracing for something difficult.

She wore a long black coat buttoned neatly over a peach and white cable-knit sweater, with dark jeans tucked into ankle boots.

There was a pause, the weight of too many years and unspoken things between them.

"Tae," she said, her voice calm but strained.

She tried giving a small smile—one that didn't quite reach her eyes.

"Hey," he replied. "I guess it's been a long time."

"Yeah… too long."

Tae ordered an iced Americano, then slid into the seat across from her.

"Do you want something?" he asked.

"No, I'm good," she said, nodding toward the half-finished cup of coffee in front of her.

As they sat, Tae found himself searching her face for traces of the teenager he'd once known. He remembered her differently.

Two years ago, when he had briefly met her at Sonia's home

in New York, she had been a freshman in college—all energy and curiosity, chatting non-stop like a firecracker during his brief visit.

She had peppered him with questions about his life in Korea, about his experiences being in Orion, about other famous Korean actors and idols.

Her laughter had been constant, and her eyes had sparkled with a kind of adolescent fervor. She was the type to speak before thinking, ready and willing to share her perspectives on anything from Bollywood to BTS.

The girl before him now seemed more subdued. Her shoulders carried a tension that hadn't been there before. The brightness in her expression had dimmed, replaced by something more solemn… more measured.

The silence stretched a moment too long.

The hum of the espresso machine in the counter behind and conversations from other patrons filled the gap.

"I wasn't sure if you would come… but I'm glad you did," she said softly, breaking the ice.

He gave a faint smile; she mirrored it.

"You look… different. Grown-up."

She gave a dry laugh. "I hope so. Freshman year me was a mess. I think I tried to get you to teach me dance routines from Orion when you visited."

Tae chuckled; the sound caught somewhere between nostalgia and sadness.

"You had more questions about my life as an idol than your sister ever did."

"I was starstruck. You were the only huge star I had ever met. That, and I was trying to get out of doing homework."

"Mission accomplished." He smiled gently.

"How's college going? Columbia, right?"

"It's okay. I'm in my junior year, majoring in journalism."

He gave a faint smile. "Suits you."

Outside, the leaves swirled in tight spirals down the sidewalk, brushing against the café window—mirroring the way their conversation kept circling around everything except what needed to be said.

"How're Dan and Usha?" he asked at last.

He'd met Sonia's parents two years ago, when she had first introduced him as her boyfriend. He'd stayed with them in their five bedroom house in upstate New York—and that day remained one of the most precious memories he had since coming to America.

In a country where he had no family, her parents had welcomed him like one of their own. Her mother, Usha, had called him *beta*—son. That first night in their home, she cooked him butter chicken and kimchi fried rice, then sat beside him at the table assuring him everything would be okay, and he didn't have to feel alone.

Tae had been particularly on edge that day—the results of his PhD comprehensive exam would come out the next morning. If he failed, it could mean the end of his doctorate degree. The weight of that uncertainty had settled heavily on his shoulders, and Usha had sensed it without needing to ask.

Dan, too, had been kind—asking about his research, listening with quiet attentiveness, and offering help if he ever needed anything.

They didn't ask questions he couldn't answer. Didn't probe into why he'd left Korea. They simply gave him space to breathe.

When it was time to leave, Usha drew him into a hug—

not out of politeness—but with the kind of warmth that said, *You matter*. His own mother's touch had always been careful, measured—never like this.

For one brief evening, he'd felt held.

Sarah exhaled, her shoulders sinking.

"Not great. Mom passed out the night we heard the news, hit her head on the floor. We rushed her to the hospital. She's in the ICU."

Tae's heart dropped. "Is she… is she okay?"

"For a while we weren't sure how bad it was," Sarah said softly. "Thankfully, she's stable now. But they're keeping her under close watch."

Tae looked down, guilt biting at his throat.

"I should've reached out."

Sarah shook her head.

"You couldn't have known. This isn't on you."

He nodded, but the words did little to soften the ache.

"How about Dan?"

She hesitated. "Dad's been… Dad. He doesn't say much, but I can tell he's struggling. He's been handling everything alone—paperwork, calls, dealing with the embassy. He's doing everything to bring her home."

Tae's throat tightened.

Bring her home.

Not Sonia, the girl who once filled any room with light.

But her body—boxed and wrapped in silence—was crossing borders.

Not a daughter. A fiancée. A sister.

Just a cargo.

A name in transit.

Neither of them spoke.

61

The silence that followed was thick and cruel.

Sarah's voice broke through it, low and trembling.

"I still can't believe she's gone. Part of me keeps expecting her to call, you know? Just text me something stupid. A meme. A cat in a sweater."

A soft, painful laugh escaped Tae, both staring down at their cups.

"She loved you," Sarah said suddenly.

"She told me... a lot of things. But that was always clear."

Tae looked away.

"I wasn't there when it mattered."

"No one knew," Sarah said quietly. "Not even us."

A beat passed before she added, "Tae, can I ask you something?"

"Of course."

"Do you know why she was in Jeju?"

He nodded slowly.

"I got an email from her. Just after..." He paused, voice catching.

"It must've been scheduled. She said she'd gone there to surprise me—for my birthday. Our anniversary too."

He pulled out his phone and handed it to Sarah.

"She even attached a plane ticket. Told me to meet her there."

Tae took a shaky breath as Sarah read through the email and watched the video.

"That explains a lot," Sarah murmured at last, almost to herself. "We thought it might've had something to do with you, but... she never told us."

"She didn't tell me either," Tae said quietly. "I only found out today."

Sarah frowned, her brows knitting together.

"The Korean authorities are calling it an accident," she said. "But I still can't wrap my head around it. It just… doesn't add up, especially after seeing the video."

He looked up. "What do you mean?"

She leaned in, her voice low but firm.

"Tae, didn't you notice… Sonia was always a little afraid of heights. Not full-on panic, but cautious. She never liked being too close to edges—even balconies made her uneasy."

Tae recalled their trip to Niagara Falls last year. Sonia had stayed inside the observatory the whole time, preferring not to go near the railing.

"In the video," Sarah continued, replaying the video, pausing on a frame. "Look—she's nowhere near the edge. See? She's standing well back, like she knows her limits."

Tae leaned closer, eyes scanning the frame.

She was right.

There was space—deliberate, cautious space—between Sonia and the cliff's edge.

Sarah sat back, arms crossed tightly over her chest.

"And now we're supposed to believe she just casually wandered up to the edge of a cliff *alone* for a selfie? And slipped? That makes no sense."

"If she went to the edge…" Sarah said, her voice dropping, "then someone must've gotten her there. *Somehow*."

Tae's jaw clenched as a slow, familiar chill crept back up his spine.

He was quiet for a moment, the weight of Sarah's words finally settling in.

He nodded slowly.

For the first time, the idea that this wasn't just a tragic accident didn't feel like paranoia. He'd dismissed the thought before, chalked it up to grief, to guilt, twisting into suspicion.

He'd gone down that path once already with Mino and ended up lost in questions no one wanted to ask—and for which there were no answers.

But this time, it felt real.

Like something he already knew, buried deep beneath the denial.

"I've been going over everything," Sarah said, her fingers tightening around her coffee cup. "And it's like something's missing. I don't know what. . . but something's off."

"And there's one more thing I need to tell you."

Tae leaned in.

"They recovered her phone," she said.

His eyes widened. "They did?"

"Yeah. They found it at the bottom of the cliff in the water, close to her body. But… here's the strange thing—it wasn't broken. Not even cracked. Just a little dirt and scuffing, but otherwise intact."

Tae blinked, confused. "Wait—how is that possible?"

"Exactly. From that height, it should've been shattered."

"Were they able to recover any data from the phone?" he asked, a thread of hope in his chest.

Sarah shook her head.

"No… apparently it was too damaged from seawater to retrieve anything. But what's even stranger—her engagement ring is missing. They didn't find it on her. And I know for a fact, she never took it off. They said maybe it slipped off during the fall… but I don't know. Still feels weird."

Tae felt his breath catch.

He had picked out that ring himself.

A slender gold band crowned with a rose-cut pink diamond,

his initials engraved inside… and hers inside his.

He instinctively reached for his band, turning it slowly against his skin as his thoughts raced.

One after another.

The pieces were lining up.

"I'm sorry to bring all this up," Sarah said quietly. "I know it's a lot. And I know it must be hard for you. But I don't have anyone else to talk to. My parents… they're barely holding on. I can't talk to them about this."

"You don't have to apologize," Tae said, meeting her eyes. "I'm glad you told me."

Sarah hesitated, then drew a slow breath.

"There's another reason I came to see you all the way from New York."

He blinked, sensing the shift in her tone.

"I want you to go to Korea," she said.

"It's a request," she added quickly, her voice more tentative now.

"I'd go myself if I could… but with Mom in the ICU, and Dad alone… I need to stay here. I'm all they have. But you"—her voice softened—"you know that world. You speak the language and understand how things work there. You might be able to find answers that I can't."

Tae stared into his coffee.

"I'm sorry to ask this of you," Sarah said. "I know it's a lot."

A pause.

He looked up.

"You don't have to apologize—I'll go," he said, his voice steadier than it had been in days.

"I also want to know what happened. I *need* to."

"Thank you…" she said, her fingers briefly wrapping around

his hand as relief washed over her face.

After they parted, Tae walked home slowly, the weight of the decision settling into his bones.

At the corner, he paused beneath the soft glow of a street-lamp and pulled out his phone.

His thumb hovered over a name he hadn't touched in years. **Yoon Hana.**

For a moment, he hesitated.

Then he pressed Call.

* * *

Mapo, Seoul

Rain tapped lightly against the windshield of a parked sedan.

The narrow streets of Mapo glistened under passing head-lights. Neon signs flickered from convenience stores and noodle shops. Music still pulsed from basement bars, and the sidewalks glowed under the haze.

Low-rise buildings—old brick and cement—stood shoulder to shoulder. Laundry lines hung from tiny balconies, and dim yellow light spilled from half-drawn curtains above.

Inside the car, Hana sat hunched in the driver's seat, method-ically chewing through her *chamchi kimbap*—rice, tuna mayo, and pickled radish wrapped in seaweed. She chewed without looking down, eyes fixed on a building entrance across the street.

At last, a man emerged from the building's front door—mid-forties, slightly balding, shirt untucked, a blazer slung casually over one shoulder.

He lit a cigarette as the door closed behind him.

A few seconds later, a woman followed, dressed in simple jeans and a cropped sweater, her hair still tousled.

They didn't speak or touch, but their body language told another story—too close, too aware of each other.

Hana sat up slightly, reaching for the camera beside her. She raised it with practiced ease, fingers adjusting the zoom as the couple stepped into frame.

Click.

Click.

The shutter snapped in quiet, deliberate bursts—sharp and precise— against the soft patter of rain on the windshield.

"Jabassda," she muttered, her eye tracking their every step.

(Got you.)

She bit into the rest of her kimbap.

Then—a soft chime.

Her phone lit up.

She glanced down, narrowing her eyes.

The name on the screen made her pause mid-bite.

Park Taejoon.

She picked up, slow, cautious.

"Beonho ajikdo isseo?"

(You still have my number?)

A pause—brief, charged.

"I'm coming back," Tae said.

"And I need to see you."

Chapter 7

NARI SAT CURLED OVER the low wooden table that served as her desk, her small body folded in like a leaf pressed between pages, knees tucked tightly beneath her.

She gripped the pencil with quiet determination, holding it steady as it hovered above the paper on the table.

Then, slowly, deliberately, she began to write:

"Dear Jiho,
How are you? Did you get my letter from last week? I hope so. I—

She paused and studied her writing, her tiny mouth forming a pout. Then immediately erased the line, rewriting it again with slow, careful strokes, making sure each letter looked neat and precise.

The afternoon light came in filtered through the only window in the apartment. Inside, the soft, steady scratch of her pencil against paper filled the silence. Beside her sat her pink pencil case with a floppy-eared rabbit character, and her worn-out backpack.

Her concentration was interrupted by the soft creak of footsteps.

Eomma entered, carrying a red pot of ramyun swaddled in folded newspaper, steam gently rising from the lid. The sharp, familiar scent of fermented chili, garlic and toasted sesame oil filled the room.

Eomma knelt down and set it on the floor, then began arranging the side dishes—kimchi, a halved boiled egg, and cold tofu in soy sauce.

She took her chopsticks and fished out a small bundle of noodles, transferring it into a chipped porcelain bowl.

"Eat before it gets cold," she instructed Nari while using her chopsticks to eat directly from the pot.

Nari reluctantly set her letter aside and picked up her chopsticks.

"What were you writing?" Eomma asked, a smile on her face.

Nari hesitated.

Eomma tilted her head, teasing.

"A letter to Jiho?"

Nari's cheeks turned pink, and she nodded.

"Can Eomma read it?"

Nari shook her head quickly, eyes big and serious.

"*Aigoo*," Eomma said with a smile, leaning in playfully.

"*Bimil?*"

(A secret?)

"Not even Eomma can know?"

Nari glanced down, her cheeks tinged peach, then gave a shy nod. Eomma chuckled, gently brushing Nari's bangs from her forehead.

"*Arasseo, arasseo.* I won't look. I'm a girl too, you know. I understand."

Her voice softened. "When you've finished writing it, just give it to me quietly. I'll mail it for you."

She picked up her chopsticks once more, lifting a strand of noodles to her lips. As she chewed slowly, her gaze unfocused, as if drifting to some distant shore.

"You know…" she said softly, almost to herself, "…your Abeoji used to write me letters too."

She chuckled.

"Back in high school. He'd tear pages from the backs of his notebooks and scribble notes for me between classes. Then, he'd slip them to me during lunch."

Nari looked up, eyes round with wonder.

Eomma smiled gently.

"Hard to imagine, isn't it? That your grumpy Abeoji was once a soft-hearted romantic—so shy, he could barely look me in the eye."

"But still he wrote me a letter every single day with ink-stained fingers."

Nari watched her mother, her gaze guarded, a flicker of doubt in her eyes.

Eomma noticed.

"You still don't believe me, do you?" she teased softly.

Without waiting for a reply, she rose and walked over to the cupboard. From its depths, she retrieved an old photo album—its edges frayed.

She returned to the floor, settled beside Nari, and opened it with care. The pages crackled faintly as she turned them, until she landed on one.

She tapped her finger against the glossy square.

"*Yogi... uriya.*"

(Here… that's us.)

In the photograph: a girl in a crisp school uniform, her hair tied in neat pigtails, her cheeks round and glowing. Beside her stood a boy, not much older, his hand resting lightly on her shoulder.

His gaze soft, almost reverent, fixed only on her.

They were both smiling—*really* smiling.

Nari stared at the picture.

Her mother and father looked so happy, like people in a movie.

It was them… but somehow, it didn't feel like them.

She wondered what happened to them.

Why didn't they smile like this anymore? When did their laughter turn into shouting?

Eomma fell quiet for a moment, the smile on her lips touched with longing.

"When I ran away from home, I could take just one small suitcase with me. I left almost everything behind. But these albums… I couldn't bear to let them go."

Her voice faded into silence, but Eomma's eyes stayed fixed on the photo, as if searching for something she had once known.

Slowly, the smile that lingered on her lips began to unravel, like a thread being pulled loose from a seam—gradually fraying as the weight of her present settled in.

Nari said nothing. She simply reached out, wordless, her small fingers gently lifting the corner of her mother's lips, as if sculpting the smile back into place.

"*Eomma, usseoyo,*" she thought.

(Mom, smile.)

71

Eomma's breath caught—just for a moment—as if emotion had risen too quickly to hide.

"*Gwaenchanha...*," she said, her voice barely above a whisper, tender and tremulous.

(I'm okay.)

"Because I have Nari. And Nari is such a good girl."

Then, as if afraid of what might spill from her heart if she lingered too long, she stood abruptly, wiping her hands on her apron with a quick, fluttering motion.

"*Yeogi isseo.*"

(Wait here.)

"I have something for you."

She returned a moment later, cradling something against her chest. She unwrapped the bundle with careful hands, unfolding it layer by layer as if revealing a secret.

A hanbok shimmered in the afternoon light—muted now by time—but still beautiful. Soft silk in shades of pale pink and ivory, embroidered with tiny blossoms along the hem.

"This was mine when I was your age," she said, her smile soft and proud.

Nari stared at the dress in awe. She couldn't look away.

The colors, the folds, the way it shimmered under the light—it was magic.

"Halmeoni embroidered every petal by hand."

Nari always knew her mother used to dance. She'd seen the photographs—tucked into the back of an old album. In one of them, Eomma wore a white hanbok, her arms stretched like wings looking like a *yojeong*, a fairy.

Eomma told her that Halmeoni, her grandmother, used to dance too—only she was even more famous. People used to call Halmeoni *Princess of the Stage* for her *Salpuri* and *Seungmu* performances.

Halmeoni and Harabeoji—Eomma's parents—were very respected, and knew lots of important people.

Nari never met them.

They were already gone before she was born.

There had been a brother too—an older sibling. But Eomma didn't talk about him much, and when she did, her voice would get very quiet, like she was remembering something too painful.

Eomma used to say she grew up in a big beautiful house in Seoul, tucked into a quiet hillside neighborhood where the cicadas sang in the summer. The doors were wooden, carved with delicate patterns.

And there was a garden in their backyard that teemed with white *mokryeon*—Korean magnolias—and purple *danhonghwa*, irises, that opened wide in the spring. Wild chrysanthemums, clustered and spilled like gold into the corners of stone pathways.

When it rained Eomma would often say that the scent of pine, would rise from the earth. And at night, blue silk lanterns hung from wooden beams, glowing softly like fireflies.

In the far corner stood a Korean zelkova tree—old and broad, with rough bark like folded paper and leaves that looked like emerald teardrops. Eomma had said it had been there since before she was born. Its branches stretched wide, and in the fall its leaves would turn copper and gold.

Also before getting married to Abeoji, Eomma never had to do any household chores. There were ajummas—middle-aged older women—who helped out: one who peeled apples and sliced persimmons for Eomma every morning, and another who kept the house all clean and sparkly.

To Nari, the house sounded like something out of a fairy tale. She always imagined her mother floating through the rooms like a princess.

Eomma was supposed to follow in Halmeoni's footsteps. But instead, she ran away with Abeoji and her family never forgave her for that. Even when they died, she wasn't allowed at their funeral.

Nari didn't understand all of it, but she knew this was something that made Eomma very sad.

Sometimes, after Eomma and Abeoji argued, Nari would peek out from the room and see her mother sitting on the floor in front of Halmeoni's picture, her back hunched, her shoulders small, voice trembling.

She always said sorry.

For being a bad daughter.

For not listening to them.

Over and over.

Like she thought Halmeoni could still hear her.

Nari reached out, her fingers grazing the soft pink fabric of the hanbok as if afraid it might vanish. It was the most beautiful thing she had ever seen. Her eyes sparkled as she traced the fine weave of the fabric, a soft shade of pink.

Pink—her favorite color.

Jinjja yeppeuda, she thought, the words echoing quietly in her mind.

(*It's really pretty.*)

She looked at Eomma, hope shining in her eyes asking: *Is it for me?*

"Of course it's for you," Eomma said, her voice softening.

She knelt again, carefully smoothing the folds of the dress.

Nari's joy spilled out in a shy smile as she hugged the dress

74

to her chest.

"Let's have you try it on," Eomma said.

"Let Eomma see how beautiful you look."

She held the hanbok open, and Nari stepped into it, eyes wide, breath held. The silk kissed her skin, clinging gently to her petite frame. The *chima*, long and flowing, wrapped around her chest and fell in elegant pleats, brushing her ankles like a breeze. The *jeogori*, the short jacket, fit delicately around her shoulders, its sleeves tapering into graceful curves that fluttered when she moved.

Golden thread glinted from the floral embroidery—plum blossoms and cranes, symbols of grace and resilience. A narrow *norigae* tassel hung from the ribbon at her waist, swaying with each breath like a secret charm.

The fabric smelled faintly of lavender and the cedar box where Eomma kept her most precious things.

Nari gave a twirl—just once—but it was enough to make the skirt flare like a blooming flower, a flurry of cherry blossoms caught in a breeze.

She laughed, dizzy with delight.

Eomma clapped her hands, joy sparkling in her eyes.

"*Anja*," she said gently, opening an old, worn tin.

(Sit.)

"Let's match your makeup to the dress."

Inside the box were little treasures from another time—crumbled bits of eyeshadow like colored dust, a half-used lipstick, and a stubby eyebrow pencil.

With the careful grace of someone handling something precious, Eomma dabbed BB cream onto Nari's cheeks, smoothing it in soft, circular motions. A sweep of shimmer brightened her eyelids. A touch of rouge brought life to her cheeks.

"Halmeoni used to do my makeup, just like this," Eomma murmured, a wistful smile touching her lips.

"Before every performance..."

And finally, with hands that trembled just slightly, she uncapped the lipstick and painted Nari's lips with slow, delicate strokes.

"Jeogi itda," she whispered. *"Yeppeuda."*

(There. So pretty.)

Nari looked into the mirror, eyes wide, as if seeing herself for the first time—stunned by how she looked.

"Can you do the dance I taught you?" Eomma asked, her voice laced with longing.

Her legs no longer moved the way they once had—worn down by time, by pain, by too many silent falls.

So, Nari danced for her.

She stepped into the open space with quiet reverence.

Her arms rose slowly, wrists curving like petals unfurling to light, her feet brushing the floor with each deliberate, floating, step.

At home, Nari would sometimes catch glimpses of Eomma—dancing quietly in the living room when she thought no one was watching.

She was the most beautiful when she danced.

The most *free.*

She moved now as Eomma once had, graceful, grounded, arms floating, feet gliding across the worn wooden floor.

In her hands, the *Salpuri* breathed again—its sorrow and strength passed down, mother to daughter, like memory.

Nari saw Eomma's gaze on her.

Her mother said nothing, but she didn't need to.

The warmth and pride reflected in her eyes.

* * *

[Suggested soundtrack: *"Love and War" by Fleurie.* Press play as this section starts.]

Somewhere, in the present—

In a dark room, another pair of eyes watched:

Tae's.

Half lit and larger than life.

His tender gaze—fixed, unblinking—stared out from a towering poster.

The space around it felt sacred, almost shrine-like.

The air was thick with the scent of *baekhyang*—Korean white sandalwood—smoky, musky, faintly floral.

Incense sticks burned down to red ash, as coils of smoke curled into the air toward the ceiling… rising like spirits being summoned from dust.

At its center, a single white candle burned: its flame tall, rigid, unnervingly still. Around it, twelve smaller red candles circled in perfect symmetry.

Their flames swayed gently, as if breathing—twelve silent witnesses—their wax pooling in dark crimson on the wooden floor.

Beneath this private altar, a figure emerged, cloaked in a red and black hanbok.

The deep crimson *chima* blazed like a flame beneath the glow of red lights. The midnight-black *jeogori*, trimmed in gold, clung to their slender frame, its silk sleeves trailing behind like smoke.

"Love and War" by Fleurie played in the background.

They began the *Salpuri*—slow, deliberate, aching with grace. Soft. Haunting. Melancholic.

The piano notes threaded through the dance like silk thread through the eye of a needle.

Born from shamanic ritual, the *Salpuri* was once danced to chase away spirits of grief: a ghost-dance of mourning and memory, offered to the wind to carry sorrow away from the soul.

The dancer's hands carved through the air, fingers curved delicately, wrists folding and unfolding with aching precision—unwrapping grief, layer by layer. Each movement echoed with restraint and release, as if peeling sorrow from the body in folds.

The hanbok fluttered with them, red and black intertwining—like fire and ash waltzing across the floor. Tears streamed down their cheeks, silent and unchecked, soaking into the silk veil that clung to their skin.

They began to twirl—slowly at first, then with growing purpose.

Arms drifting at their sides, head tilted,

as if listening for something only they could hear.

Around and around, they spun—

rhythmic, dreamlike—

like a child rocked gently by an unseen force.

A soundless sob racked through them, but the motion didn't stop.

It deepened.

Became a trance.

A lullaby of grief and longing,

played for an audience of one.

From above, Tae's image looked down—

eyes wide, fixed in eternal stillness—
like a god summoned to bear witness to his own worship.
The dancer twirled one final time,
and in that breathless motion,
a glint caught the light.
A pink diamond.
Shimmering like a secret on their finger,
its dazzling brilliance shadowed
by the faintest sliver of blood.

Chapter 8

T AE STEPPED ONTO THE plane, the cool, recycled air brushing against his face.

A single backpack hung off one shoulder—his only carry-on. He had already checked in his main suitcase at the terminal, so while other passengers shuffled in with suitcases and garment bags, Tae stood quietly near the entrance, unencumbered.

He glanced down at his boarding pass—his name, **TAEJOON PARK**, printed in bold across the top.

Near the bottom, in crisp, unmistakable letters: *First Class*.

He had planned to book economy, something quiet and low-profile. But of course, the seat had already been arranged by his brother.

That was Minjae for you—always one step ahead, always looking out for him, whether he asked for it or not.

When Tae mentioned he was coming back, he got an immediate text from Minjae:

"What day?"

When Tae replied that he hadn't booked his ticket yet, Minjae followed up almost instantly:

"Hyung-i haejulgae."

(Let your hyung handle it.)

That was it. No discussion. No room to argue.

Just Minjae, steady as always, taking care of things in the background like he always had.

As he stepped past the threshold, a flight attendant greeted him with a courteous smile.

"*Annyeonghasaeyo*. May I see your ticket?"

(Hello.)

He handed it to her without a word. She glanced at it, then gestured politely down the aisle.

"Please continue this way."

He murmured his thanks and moved through the narrow aisle of first class, leather seats gleaming under soft ambient light.

As Tae passed by, one of the flight attendants offered him a polite smile and slight bow.

Behind her, another leaned toward her colleague, whispering just loud enough for him to catch.

"*Jal saeng-gyeotda... idol aniya?*"

(He's good-looking... maybe an idol?)

The first attendant stifled a grin, then leaned slightly to get a better look at his face.

"*Molla...*"

(Not sure.)

Tae kept his gaze forward, pretending not to hear, his face neutral. He scanned the rows, spotting his number near the front.

11 A.

Sliding into his window seat, he exhaled slowly. The cushions were plush, but he felt no comfort. He glanced at the empty seat beside him.

Sonia would always take the aisle.

She liked to stretch her legs and people-watch when they flew.

"It's strategic," she'd tease with a grin. "I see the food coming before you do, and I don't have to wake you up every time I need the bathroom."

He could still hear her voice in that gentle, teasing lilt—the warmth of it still clear, as if she were beside him now.

He turned his face toward the window, eyes drifting over the still tarmac, where service trucks crawled and runway lights blinked in quiet rhythm.

He stared without really seeing, trying not to remember, wanting the hours to pass, willing the ache to loosen its grip... if only for a few hours.

Just then, someone tapped him lightly on the shoulder.

He opened his eyes to see an older Korean woman standing beside him, her small frame slightly stooped, a soft lavender cardigan buttoned neatly over her blouse.

Her face, lined with soft wrinkles and framed by wisps of graying hair, held a quiet kindness.

A large black suitcase stood beside her—clearly too heavy for her to lift on her own.

"*Jeogiyo... mianhande*," she said, glancing slightly toward her suitcase.

(Excuse me... sorry.)

"*Geureo deurilgeyo*," Tae said politely, already rising from his seat.

(Of course, I'll help you with that.)

He reached up and lifted the modest roller bag into the overhead compartment with practiced ease.

She smiled up at him.

"*Aigoo, gomawoyo*."

82

(Goodness, thank you.)

Tae offered a small, respectful nod, already sinking back into his seat.

She settled beside him with a grateful sigh.

As the plane taxied, Tae scrolled to a message blinking on his phone from his brother:

"Bame jal tteona."

(Have a safe flight.)

"Don't forget to call as soon as you land."

He smiled. Years had passed, but some things hadn't changed at all. His hyung still treated him like a kid.

Another message blinked in—this one from Roger.

The photo showed Roger smiling wide, arm draped around Lola, who sat beside him with her nose pointed stubbornly in the other direction, like she wanted absolutely nothing to do with him.

"Besties hanging out," he wrote, emoji-filled and proudly captioned.

Tae shook his head and chuckled.

Classic Roger.

Even so, his chest loosened a little.

He was thankful Roger had stepped up to take care of Lola without hesitation. He wasn't someone with a long list of friends. He kept his circle small. But Roger had always been there when it mattered, and for that he was grateful.

Tae glanced over and caught the older woman staring him. He wondered if she recognized him.

"Neo eolguli…" she said after a moment, tilting her head.

(Your face…)

Tae offered a modest smile, bracing for her to recognize him from Orion.

83

"Ah! Algess-eo!"

(I know!)

"Uri Jib Mujigae! Jiho, geoji?"

(Rainbow Family—You're Jiho, right?)

He chuckled softly, surprised anyone could still recognize him from when he was a child actor. That had been nearly twenty years ago.

"Ne, majayo," he replied politely with a practiced laugh.

(Yes, that's right.)

She went on to say how her children had loved the show—how they never missed a single episode. With a laugh, she recalled how her son used to get annoyed whenever she compared him to Jiho.

"Why can't you be sweet like him?" she'd scold.

Her son had hated it.

Tae was used to it.

Over the years, countless parents had come up to him, saying the same thing—how they saw Jiho as the perfect boy. The ideal son. The media had even dubbed him *"Korea's son."*

But Tae had long grown tired of playing that part.

Jiho was always smiling. Even when others hurt him, he bore it quietly, with grace. Never angry. Never sad. Never allowed to feel anything real. Just endlessly cheerful.

There was nothing authentic about the character. And Tae couldn't understand how anyone found Jiho relatable.

In time, he began to resent the role. He'd begged his mother to let him quit. And for a brief moment, she agreed—seeing how unhappy he was.

But his popularity was too strong, and the production company refused to release him.

So he kept playing Jiho—an eight-year-old boy—even as he

crossed into double digits.

It wasn't until he hit a growth spurt at thirteen—towering over the rest of the cast and unable to squeeze into his elementary school uniform—that they finally took notice.

But even then, their solution wasn't to let him go. Instead, they rewrote the script, added a time skip, and sent Jiho to middle school.

"Ahn Kyung-seok-ssi—" the woman said, her voice cutting into Tae's thoughts.

"Do you remember him? That actor… he played your appa on *Uri Jib Mujigae,* right?"

"*Ne, majayo,*" Tae said, nodding with a polite smile.

(Yes, that's right.)

She laughed softly. "*Jinjja, geu saram johasseo.*"

(Honestly, I had such a crush on him.)

"He was so handsome," she continued, her voice tinged with nostalgia.

"Even more handsome than my husband—bless his soul"

She leaned in slightly, lowering her voice.

"What was he like on set?"

Tae gave a diplomatic smile, his tone measured.

"He was very kind. Very professional. I learned a lot from him."

She nodded, clearly pleased with the answer.

"That's good. You always hear people say 'never meet your idols,' right? I never got to meet him—but I'm glad to know he really was that kind."

Tae smiled, but he knew the truth was far less pretty.

Ahn Kyung-seok and Seo Hye-jin—the actress who played Tae's mother—could barely stand to be in the same room once the cameras stopped.

They were a real-life couple teetering on the brink of divorce.

To the nation, they were the perfect family.

In truth, they were held together by little more than makeup, lighting, and contractual obligation.

Each time the cameras rolled, they stepped into roles they no longer believed in. Their marriage was a performance long past curtain call—their bitterness leaking into every gesture, every forced smile on set, making everyone around them walk on eggshells.

It didn't help that Ahn Kyung-seok was extremely possessive and volatile.

Rumors swirled on set about his explosive temper, though rumors weren't necessary. The bruises on Seo Hye-jin's face and body told their own story: the faint swelling on her cheek behind oversized sunglasses, the purplish shadow on her arm masked beneath careful layers of concealer.

Anything could set him off—her laughing too easily with a male staff member, failing to tell him about a meeting with a co-star, greeting the director too warmly, or even giving too much attention to a child.

Tae had experienced that last one firsthand.

Seo Hye-jin, his on-screen mother, had always been gentle with him in a way that felt genuinely maternal: encouraging him, complimenting his performance, straightening his collar between scenes, occasionally slipping him candy or little treats.

But even those simple acts of affection seemed to provoke her husband.

Overtime, Ahn Kyung-seok had grown cold toward Tae, often ignoring him between takes. As a child, Tae hadn't understood it—the tension on set, the sudden hush that fell once the director called "cut," or the way the air changed when the cameras stopped rolling.

He remembered one scene vividly. His character, Jiho, was meant to be scolded by his father for lying. The script called for a raised voice, a dramatic pause, and a staged slap.

But Ahn Kyung-seok didn't pretend.

The slap landed—sharp, sudden, real.

The set fell into stunned silence as Tae's cheek flared red with the imprint of a hand that was never meant to touch him.

His mother, Yura, intervened at once. She demanded an apology, threatened legal action if necessary. And given her stature as both a legendary actress and wife of a chaebol heir, Ahn Kyung-seok had little choice but to comply.

He offered the apology—stiff, hollow and devoid of regret.

Thankfully, he never touched Tae again. But it did nothing to ease the tension on set.

His bitterness lingered, simmering beneath the surface—now directed at others, particularly those in lower-ranking positions.

In the end, it wasn't his temper that ended the show.

It was scandal.

Ahn Kyung-seok was caught by members of the production team having an affair on set with Jung Sae-mi, a supporting actress who had joined the cast in a later season.

She played Jiho's noona—his character's older half-sister, the daughter from their father's first marriage.

The revelation was unthinkable.

Rainbow Family had come to symbolize the ideal Korean household—a warm, wholesome portrait of love, virtue, and belonging.

For viewers to learn that the man who played the gentle, selfless father had been involved with the actress who portrayed his daughter was scandal enough.

But Jung Sae-mi was only sixteen.

A high school student. A child.

Ahn Kyung-seok was forty-five.

The affair wasn't just immoral—it was repugnant.

And for Korean viewers, who regarded Ahn Kyung-seok as the embodiment of fatherhood, it was *yongseohal su eopda*—a stain no apology could erase, a sin beyond forgiveness.

The production team acted swiftly, releasing Ahn Kyung-seok from the show before the story could explode. And for Seo Hye-jin, it was the final blow.

Within days, she filed for divorce.

Tae glanced at the older woman seated beside him, now asleep, her head tilted gently toward the aisle, hands folded in her lap.

He smiled faintly. *She didn't need to know the truth.*

For her—and likely for the remainder of her life—Ahn Kyung-seok would remain the dashing, dignified father and faithful husband she had admired on screen.

And Tae didn't have the heart to shatter that illusion.

He reached for the screen and absently scrolled through the in-flight entertainment, half-seeing the titles as they slid past—until one caught his eye.

Revenge Sonata.

Jaeho's latest series. The one Roger had offhandedly recommended.

Tae stilled.

Jaeho. Orion's *maknae*—the youngest member.

The lead rapper and dancer, and, unofficially, its second visual—though some fans argued Jaeho eclipsed Tae in sheer magnetism. In K-pop terms, the "visual" wasn't just the best-looking member: it was the face of the group, the one meant to leave a first impression, to captivate at a glance.

At five feet, ten inches, Jaeho was a designer's dream with a lean, athletic dancer's build and a versatile aesthetic from soft romantic to sleek high-fashion runaway looks. He moved through fashion like water. His image was endlessly mutable.

The modeling campaigns followed naturally. Then came the acting roles. Small ones, at first—a few bit roles here and there. *Revenge Sonata* was his first lead in a global series.

Tae hesitated for a moment, thumb hovering over the screen.

Then he pressed play.

And there he was.

Jaeho, once the bright-eyed boy with stars in his eyes, now stood on-screen as a man—poised, magnetic and devastating. His eyes, once wide and eager, now carried the weight of buried intensity.

He said little in the first scene, but Tae couldn't look away.

His silences held weight, pulsing with meaning. His expressions shifted with the subtlety of tides—minute, controlled, restrained.

He was good.

Really good.

It was strange, watching him now, inhabiting a world so far from the mirror-lined rehearsal rooms they once shared. It was hard to reconcile this commanding presence with the boy who used to follow Tae around like a shadow, desperate to keep up.

A part of Tae felt proud. Another part felt heavy—with guilt.

He hadn't spoken to any of them since leaving Korea.

As the episode played on, his mind began to wander. He

wondered about the other members and how they were doing.

He remembered Rian who was the same age as him.

Rian, who had always seemed born for the camera. His presence had a rare, liquid charisma, a presence that was easy, practiced, without ever feeling forced. The kind that made strangers lean in, want to hear more.

He stood at five foot nine, lean but polished, with a bright smile and the easy confidence of someone used to being watched. His features were clean-cut—slightly upturned eyes that glinted with amusement or calculation, a perfectly cut nose, and a mouth that knew exactly when to smile.

His style was mercurial—one day tousled and boyish in a sweatshirt and jeans, the next day sleek, statuesque and swept back in bone-white suits and silk shirts. He shifted seamlessly between boy next door charm and sharp ambition. His laugh was easy, frequent. His phone never stopped buzzing.

Rian had always been the sun, the social prince, the butterfly of the group. The charismatic charmer, the connector, the crowd pleaser among all the group members—the one who knew how to make any one feel like the only person in the room.

The last Tae heard, Rian was happily married. To a su-permodel. A former Miss Korea contestant. They had two children, and Rian had parlayed his popularity into becoming an owner of a lifestyle empire—luxury spas, night clubs, rooftop bars, and five-star restaurants with waiting lists two months long.

Tae saw it as a natural evolution for Rian.

The spotlight had shifted, but Rian still knew how to dazzle. This new life—as a business mogul—fit him like a tailored suit.

Then there was Duri.

The eldest. The group's leader and main vocalist.

Duri moved like someone born in another century in a way that blended elegance and restraint: tall, austere, and graceful. At over six feet, he carried himself with an air of quiet power like a statue carved from marble and bathed in light. His face was all sharp lines and elegant shadow: cheekbones that could cut glass, a long, aristocratic nose, and eyes that held a cool, distant gaze, that drew attention without asking for it.

He wore bold, tailored coats in deep velvet and structured wool, choosing each piece like a curator assembling a private gallery. And his voice, when he used it, rumbled low, like distant thunder—measured, poetic, and commanding.

There was something deliberate in everything he did—from the way he adjusted his cufflinks to how he let silence settle before answering a question. Many mistook his silence for arrogance. But Tae had seen past it.

It wasn't pride. It was vulnerability—extreme shyness.

Out of all of them, Duri had the hardest time being an idol. He struggled the most with fame. He hated interviews, loathed press tours, froze during fan meets, rarely smiled unless instructed. And despite all the love fans gave him, he kept his distance—shunning attention, avoiding the spotlight whenever he could.

When the cameras turned off, he retreated into his sketchbook and paintings. His art was intricate, lonely, introspective.

And while he had never been one to talk much—when he did speak, everyone listened.

That's why it had been such a shock when after Mino's death, Duri, usually so contained, exploded on him.

"He called you," he had shouted, his whole body shaking. "You knew he wasn't okay. You *knew*—and yet you did nothing!"

"You're selfish Tae. You always were. This… this is on *you*. You're responsible for this."

Tae was taken aback, stunned, gutted. Of all the voices in the aftermath, Duri's cut the deepest. He'd already spent days spiraling in silence, torturing himself with what-ifs. But hearing Duri say it out loud, that *he* was to blame, felt like confirmation.

It broke something in him.

That had been the last time they spoke.

Shortly after, Tae had packed his life into a suitcase and boarded a plane for America.

The memory made his chest tighten, as though a hand had reached through time to clutch at his heart.

He had no idea how Duri was doing now.

Unlike the others, he never surfaced in the news.

The screen in front of him flickered. The episode was still playing, but he wasn't watching anymore. He closed his eyes, hoping for sleep. But it came in fits, drifting in and out— restless and shallow.

When he finally awoke he felt something soft against his shoulder. For a moment, warmth surged through him. For one aching moment, he imagined it was Sonia—her head against him the way she used to.

He turned.

It was the older woman beside him, fast asleep, her breath light and even.

The lights above dimmed, casting the cabin in a hush of midnight blue. And the plane began its descent.

Outside the window, the sky had darkened to ink.

Seoul glittered below like a spilled constellation.

He was back.

* * *

Stepping off the AREX train, Tae emerged into the grand, sun-drenched concourse of *Incheon International Airport, Terminal 1.*

Light poured through panes of glass, cascading across polished floors that shimmered beneath the movement of rolling suitcases and shifting feet.

All around him, the soundscape of arrivals and departures played like a symphony: the low murmur of conversations in Korean, English, Japanese, Mandarin; the mechanical trill of announcements; the hollow clack of suitcase wheels trailing behind weary travelers.

Counters stretched across the terminal in endless rows—some manned by flight attendants in pressed uniforms offering gentle bows and warm, practiced greetings:

"*Annyeonghaseyo. Eoseo oseyo.*"

(Hello. Welcome in.)

Duty-free stores glowed from the sides like portals, stocked with lacquered shelves of luxury cosmetics, magazines, K-beauty serums, bottles of soju in collector's packaging, glossy tins of Pepero, and towering pyramids of gimbap snack packs.

Beneath it all, signs in Hangul and English pointed in every direction—

Immigration | Baggage Claim | Nap Zones | Prayer Room—

guiding the ebb and flow of bodies through this transit cathedral.

To Tae, it felt like nothing had changed.

93

And yet, everything had.

Past immigration. Through customs. Past baggage claim. Towards the exit. The crowd surged around him like a tide, waves of people breaking in every direction.

Suddenly, he caught a flash of movement in the distance—an excited ripple through the crowd gathered at the far end of the arrivals hall. A handful of paparazzi jostled near the barriers, lenses raised, voices calling out indistinctly in Korean.

He watched with mild curiosity as a lean boy emerged from the terminal exit. A few security staff formed a makeshift cordon, but it wasn't enough to stop the wave of girls rushing forward—eyes wide, phones stretched high above their heads, voices rising in chorus.

It was a familiar scene.

He remembered how it used to be for him.

The moment he would step out of immigration, past the final checkpoint—it would begin.

The swell. The surge.

Phones flying up.

Light flashing.

Girls pressing in too close, their voices high and trembling.

"*Annoyeonhaseyo.*"

(Hello.)

"*Oppa, saranghae!*"

(Love you, Oppa.)

He was usually always flanked on all sides by his manager, a suited bodyguard, and someone else from staff trailing behind. But sometimes they were so tightly packed it felt like they might merge into him—like the crowd itself might swallow him whole.

Their energy was tidal. Overwhelming.

More than once, he had seen his bodyguard stiffen, stepping forward to block someone getting too close. His manager's voice would cut through the noise—firm, polite, practiced.

"Joesonghamnida, jom meolli isseojuseyo."

(Sorry, but please give him some space.)

The media photographers would be stationed just outside the terminal doors, fingers poised on their shutters, waiting to catch that perfect shot.

Within hours, their clips would be up online, dissected frame by frame. And the comments would come pouring in, usually accompanied by a string of emojis:

> *"Oppa dashi watda."*
> (Oppa's back again.)

> *"Yeongwonhi nae pyeon-iya."*
> (You'll forever be mine.)

> *"Taejoon-oppa, cham jal saenggyeotda…"*
> (Taejoon-oppa, you're really handsome…)

> *"Wa achim-inde butgineun keonyeong bichinajana!!"*
> (Wow, it's morning and there's not a hint of puffiness—he's glowing!!)

> *"Narang gateun raunji-e isseotgo simjilo gateun bihaenggi. Ge jal saenggyeosseum."*
> (He was in the same lounge as me and even on the same flight. He's insanely handsome.)

"Naneun Taejoon-ui gyeonghowoni doego sipda."
(I want to be Taejoon's bodyguard.)

Looking at the chaos unfold now, he felt no pang of longing. Just quiet amusement.

Then, just beyond the blur of motion, a voice cut through.
"Tae doryunnim."
(Young master Tae.)
Soft. Formal. Familiar.
He turned.
There stood Secretary Choi.

He looked almost exactly as Tae remembered him—immaculate in a charcoal suit, polished shoes gleaming under the terminal lights.

But time had brushed against him gently.

The once-jet-black hair was now threaded with silver. His posture remained proud, but his shoulders carried a quiet stoop. The hands that had always been folded with precision now trembled ever so slightly at the fingertips.

But the eyes—those sharp, alert eyes—were unchanged.
Steady. Watchful. Kind.
Tae smiled faintly. *"Choi samchon."*
(Secretary Choi).
Secretary Choi's face eased, a faint trace of relief.
He offered a small, respectful bow.
"Jincha gajimalkke."
(Let me take your luggage.)
Tae shook his head gently.
"Naega deulgeyo."
(I've got it.)

But Choi's voice grew firmer, still polite.

"Gwaenchanhseubnida. Naega halgeyo."

(It's alright. I'll do it.)

The air outside Incheon was warm and heavy with early summer heat: thick with humidity and the constant hum of arrivals and departures.

A sleek black limousine idled at the curb, its tinted windows glinting under the afternoon sun.

Just as Tae stepped toward the car, he heard it—

Click.

A shutter snapping somewhere in the crowd.

His body tensed.

He didn't need to turn. He already knew.

A low murmur rippled through the crowd.

Someone pointed. Phones began to rise.

Tae tugged the brim of his cap low, slipped a black mask over his face, and without a word, slid into the car. The door closed behind him with a soft, final **thunk.**

Inside it was quiet and still.

The faint scent of Polo Blue lingered in the air—cool ocean breeze, soft suede, a touch of musk and basil—subtle but unmistakable.

Across from him, seated in the far corner of the cabin, was his brother. Navy-blue suit. Starched white shirt. Tie knotted clean and sharp. Silver-rimmed glasses perched on the bridge of his nose. His hair, neatly parted to the side, hadn't changed since his university days. He looked like he'd stepped straight out of a board meeting.

"Hyung."

Minjae looked up, his expression unreadable save for the faintest smile tugging at the edges of his otherwise impassive face.

Still immaculate. Still painfully put together.

He gave a small nod. Then, quietly—

"Taejoon-ah... welcome back."

A beat later, softer—

"*Wassne.*"

There was a trace of warmth in the word—subtle, unspoken—just enough to reveal what he couldn't bring himself to say out loud.

(You came.)

Chapter 9

THE ONE-BEDROOM APARTMENT IN Mapo-gu sat nestled on the fourth floor of a brick building, its facade aged but clean, with ivy curling around the rust-colored banisters.

There was no elevator—only a narrow stairwell with scuffed steps, echoing with the occasional footsteps of neighbors. The smell of drying laundry drifted faintly through the hallway.

Outside, the late afternoon sun spilled over quiet residential streets lined with gingko trees that rustled above corner cafés and tucked-away convenience stores.

Inside, Hana's apartment was modest, functional, every inch shaped by necessity.

A small genkan led to a compact open space where the kitchen, dining, and living area blurred into one another. The pale cream walls, once a bright cream, had dulled over time—smudged with faint marks from old calendars and tape-peeled corners. The floors were polished wood, darkened with age, and gleamed softly in the light.

It was silent inside, broken only by the low hum of a vacuum gliding across the wood, steady, almost meditative.

Hana moved through the space with quiet precision, like a metronome—each motion measured, each swipe of her hand calculated.

"*Hana... dul... set.*"

(One... two... three.)

A short pause.

The vacuum stops for a beat, then starts again.

"*Net... daseot... yeoseot.*"

(Four... five... six.)

Another pause.

Her fingers tighten slightly on the handle as the nozzle dips beneath the couch, grazing the hidden area beneath the radiator.

"*Ilgop... yeodeol... ahop.*"

(Seven... eight... nine.)

Only then does she exhale—just a little. The pattern was complete, for now.

This wasn't just cleaning: it was a ritual.

Precision. Repetition. Devotion.

Each count kept chaos at bay, kept the intrusive thoughts folded tightly like laundry in a drawer. If she did it right—*exactly* right—nothing would fall apart.

Yoon Hana stood at five feet four, her frame slim, with shoulder-length dark hair rolled neatly into a low bun—tight, deliberate, not a strand out of place. She wore black leggings and a fitted black long-sleeved tee. Her fingernails were neatly clipped, unpolished, as precise and bare as the rest of her.

Everything about her radiated control—efficient and unmistakably tidy—except for her socks, pale green and patterned with tiny cartoon turtles, which quietly betrayed her softer side.

She now guided the vacuum into the living area that doubled as a study and sleeping space. A foldable floor mattress was rolled and secured with military precision in the corner. Beside it stood a short bookcase—every title aligned perfectly by genre and spine height. Criminal psychology textbooks came first, followed by forensic pathology references, then court transcripts from famous trials, and finally surveillance equipment manuals.

Each book was dusted and spaced evenly, as if any disruption might throw the whole system into disarray.

Next to it, a single low armchair—threadbare but clean—faced a small wall-mounted TV and a narrow window that let in slanted afternoon light.

Everything in the room had its place. Remote controls stacked symmetrically. Blankets folded in thirds. A laundry drying rack stood near the window with exactly six socks clipped in neat pairs: each one arranged by color, then by height.

Hana paused and wiped her brow, the edge of her sleeve grazing her temple as a streak of sunlight streamed across her face. Her skin was clear and pale, with a dusting of faint freckles across the bridge of her nose—catching the light like powdered gold. Her cheekbones were high, not sharp but softly defined, lending her an air of quiet resilience.

Just beneath her right eye, near the outer edge, sat a solitary beauty mark, small, perfectly placed, like an accent in a painter's final stroke. It complemented her most striking feature: her eyes.

Dark brown and clear as morning tea, her eyes held a kind of lucid intensity. Set slightly wide apart, they lent her an owl-like gaze that missed nothing.

Einstein, her turtle, blinked slowly, watching from inside his tank, perched atop his usual stone. His dark green shell shimmered faintly under the light, patterned with swirls of olive and amber from a recent misting.

Thin yellow stripes traced the length of his neck and legs, but it was the vivid red slash behind each eye—like war paint—that marked him unmistakably as a "red eared slider."

He shifted slightly, claws scratching lightly against the stone, and tilted his head, as if assessing her with quiet, ancient judgment.

Hana glanced at him with an affectionate gaze, her lips curling into a smile—one that lit her face up like a secret sunrise.

"*Nal pyeongga haj?*" Hana said softly.

(You judging me?)

"*Neodo kkaekkeutan geo joahajanha.*"

(You like it clean too.)

The scents of baking chocolate and caramelizing sugar drifted in from the kitchen, rich and inviting, as a batch of cookies rose in the oven.

Her kitchenette was narrow—just enough room for one person to cook. The cabinets were plain white, edged with peeling laminate, and the fridge bore a neat grid of sticky notes, receipts, and a single photo of a turtle in a straw hat.

She checked the timer: *exactly* three minutes left.

Just enough time to wipe down the countertops—three swipes, then six, then nine—her hands moving with compulsive precision, chanting the numbers like a prayer, chasing calm through the soothing symmetry of arithmetic.

Her obsession with perfection had its roots, buried deep—like so many things—in childhood.

Her mother had been left to raise her alone, a woman weathered by broken promises and quiet seething regrets. The man who once promised her marriage and vows of forever had disappeared long before Hana's first birthday, leaving behind a child whose face resembled his. Her mother never forgave the man who left—nor the child he left behind, who looked too much like him.

Hana had learned early that her mother couldn't look at her for long. Not without a quiet resentment flickering in her eyes.

She still remembered the sound of her mother's voice—flat, cool, and always just a little too calm, like frost settling over something that had once burned. There was cruelty in that quiet, as if every word had been dulled not to soothe, but to wound.

"Ajikdo deo kkaekkeutaji anha."

(It's still not clean.)

"Dasi haejwa. Jalte hae."

(Do it again. Do it properly.)

And so she did—again and again—scrubbing until her arms ached, until her fingers went raw.

But no matter how hard Hana tried, nothing was ever quite good enough. Her mother never seemed satisfied with anything she did. Never said the words she longed to hear.

When Hana was nine, her mother flew to Australia, a new bride chasing old dreams and brighten skies.

Hana remained behind in Korea, left in the care of her aunt and grandmother, with nothing but a small suitcase and a fragile hope of reunion that refused to let go.

Days turned to months. Seasons turned to silence.

Her mother never returned for her.

Eventually, Hana stopped checking the window.

The timer beeped.

A moment later, the oven chimed—soft and cheerful—announcing her cookies were ready.

Hana slipped on her mitts, emerald green with a dainty little turtle stitched into the corner. She opened the door, inhaling deeply.

A wave of warm, sugary air rose to greet her.

She pulled out the tray and examined the batch: chocolate chip cookies, golden at the edges, soft at the center—each one perfectly shaped. Exactly as they should be.

Baking brought the same comfort as cleaning.

Precision. Predictability. Perfection.

The recipe told her what to do, and she obeyed. In a world of constantly changing variables, a measuring cup offered no surprises—only safety.

Her friends in college used to tease her that given her baking skills she would make a perfect housewife. She'd laughed it off. But after one failed relationship in college, she never dated again. Maybe she just didn't want to be let down again.

After graduation, armed with a dual major in English and Psychology, she joined the police force. She'd always been drawn to true crime stories, fascinated by the darker corners of human behavior. Becoming a detective had felt like a way to bring light into that darkness.

To right wrongs. To protect. To serve.

But reality rarely matched the fantasy.

The hierarchy within the force was rigid, political—a lattice of rank, reputation, and silence. Decisions flowed from the top down, and those at the bottom were expected to fall in line.

Obey first. Question never.

She still remembers the case.

The one that unraveled her.

The final case that made her walk away from the force for good.

She'd only been a junior detective then—sharp instincts, tireless work ethic, but no real authority. A well-known young woman had come forward accusing her ex-boyfriend of something terrible.

No one believed her.

Not the officers. Not her superiors.

The accused was influential, well-connected.

He had the face of someone raised right—the kind people smiled at without thinking. To the public, he was everyone's son: gentle, gracious, incapable of the crime he was accused of.

They called the girl unstable. Attention-seeking. Delusional.

But Hana had believed her.

She'd seen the tremor in her hands, the fear behind her eyes. Something had happened—she knew it.

So she started digging.

Quietly. Carefully.

Pulling records, mapping timelines, questioning witnesses.

And she was getting close—very close.

Then came the call.

Cool. Flat.

From higher up.

Drop the case. Let it go.

And just like that, her hands were bound.

A few days later, she came across the girl's Instagram story.

A silent video—just her face.

There was something in her eyes Hana couldn't shake.

They were unfocused, adrift—like she was floating just

105

beyond reach.

That night, Hana sent her a message.

"Gwaenchanha?"

(Are you okay?)

No reply at first. So she sent another:

"Eotteon iri isseodo... jeongmal, jal saraya dwae."

(Whatever happens... you really have to live well.)

A few minutes later, the girl responded:

"Ung... geurae. Jal salge. Gomawo, unni."

(Yeah... I will. I'll live well. Thank you, unni.)

The next day, her body was found—

lifeless in her apartment.

Hana had never forgotten the look in her eyes from that video.

A week later, she resigned.

There was nothing left to say.

Nothing left to fight for.

Hana stepped out of the kitchen, tray in hand with the scent of fresh cookies trailing behind her.

On the table, her camera sat exactly where she'd left it the night before, beside a neat stack of printed photos—black and white—but sharp enough to leave no room for denial.

She set the tray down, wiped her hands on a dish towel, and picked up her phone.

"Sajin dasseo."

(Got the photos.)

"Dangsin nampyeon, geurigo geu yeoja."

(Your husband—and the woman he's seeing.)

She hit Send and let out a slow breath.

This was her life now.

She worked as a private investigator. Catching cheating

spouses. Shadowing teenagers for anxious parents—hoping to confirm if their son had a girlfriend or their daughter was secretly dating. Sometimes it was corporate: employees faking sick leave, slipping away to golf courses or love motels. Other times, more personal—a matrimonial agency or a nervous, soon-to-be mother-in-law requesting a discreet background check.

Nothing too messy. Nothing that left blood or guilt.

And never anything that came too close to the past.

Her phone notification chimed.

A message from Tae.

"Nado watda. mannil su isseulkka?"

(I'm here. Can we meet?)

Her fingers hovered over the screen for a beat as if weighing the reply—then, instead, she reached for another cookie.

Outside, the first drops of rain began to fall.

Chapter 10

THE SEOUL RAIN TRACED delicate paths down the floor-to-ceiling windows of the Gangnam penthouse, like ink seeping through rice paper.

Each droplet descended with hushed reverence, as if the glass itself were sacred.

Beyond the pane, Tae stepped out into the evening, beneath the awning of the covered balcony. The warm, earthy scent of petrichor drifted up from the rain-soaked rooftops and planters below, lifted by a gentle breeze.

Ahead of him, Seoul lay sprawled in every direction—a luminous organism, restless and alive—stitched together by blinking towers, traffic arteries, and the pale silver ribbon of the Han River.

Bridges throbbed with light, red and white in a hypnotic rhythm, while digital billboards shimmered and pulsed against the rain-slick facades of Gangnam's skyline.

From the uppermost floor of one of the district's most exclusive residential towers, Tae watched it all unfold below.

He pulled out his phone and opened KakaoTalk.

The message to Hana sat there: *read*, but unanswered.

He lit a cigarette with steady hands, the tip flaring briefly in the dark.

After Sonia, the habit had returned—uninvited, but familiar.

These days, he told himself it helped him focus; gave his mind something to anchor to when everything else felt like it was slipping.

Inside, the apartment—too vast and opulent for his tastes—felt overwhelming.

The ceilings soared upward, timber-beamed and backlit with warm, adjustable gold-toned lighting. The floors were Italian marble, each slab uniquely veined like rivers in stone, and the walls were adorned with abstract pieces by artists Tae had never heard of.

A curved ivory sectional cradled a sunken conversation pit like a crescent moon, and in one corner, a glossy black Steinbach baby grand rested in quiet elegance beside a row of indoor ficus trees—lush, symmetrical, pristine—as if lifted straight from a designer showroom.

It was a cathedral of wealth, a luxury cocoon carved from glass and stone, perched high above the city and sealed off from everything else.

Tae hadn't chosen this. He'd booked a relatively modest suite at a hotel in Sinsa—an upscale neighborhood in Gangnam, known for its tree-lined streets, indie boutiques, and cafés. It was the kind of place young professionals went to be seen, but was easy enough to disappear into if you knew where to stay.

But Minjae had overridden him.

"You'll stay here," he had said the night Tae arrived.

"Top floor's empty. And it's safer."

Chae Group, their family's conglomerate, owned most of the buildings in this part of Gangnam. Tae knew this. But what surprised him wasn't that Minjae had found him a place to stay—it was that he had chosen this building, his own residence, for Tae to stay in.

He had even gone so far as to assign Secretary Choi, their most trusted and senior family aide, to personally oversee every detail concerning Tae.

Minjae wasn't one for sentiment. So if he was going this far, Tae knew—his brother was genuinely worried.

Out of the corner of his eye, Tae noticed Yujin, the housekeeper, gathering her things to leave. She was twenty-four— polite, professional, but clearly nervous when she first met him.

Her voice had trembled slightly as she asked, almost shyly, if he was really *that* Taejoon from Orion.

"Geunyang... han ttae geuraetji," he had replied.

(I used to be.)

As she departed, she bowed three times, mumbling that it was an honor to clean for him.

Tae returned her gesture with a grateful smile and a word of thanks.

With Yujin gone, he'd have the place to himself.

Aside from Chef Hwan and Secretary Choi, she was one of the only people allowed access to this apartment. Tae had made sure of that.

He'd made it very clear to Minjae that he did not want an entourage. No staff rotating in shifts. No assistants hovering like shadows the way they always had in the main house.

"I'm used to living alone in Pittsburgh," he'd told him. "Having people always around… it's suffocating."

Minjae had looked surprised at his request for privacy. But he hadn't argued.

Growing up at the Chae family's main residence in Hannam-dong, often called the Beverly Hills of Seoul, privacy was a luxury even wealth couldn't buy. Their estate—a sprawling compound nestled inside the exclusive UN Village—was an architectural masterpiece of polished marble and white limestone—modern, gleaming, and expansive.

Inside, it functioned like a palace.

Staff moved with quiet precision: Maids in pressed uniforms dusted invisible specks from already spotless surfaces, chefs prepared meals to rigid schedules, and security guards with earpieces were stationed discreetly at all entry points.

To an outsider, it was perfection.

To Tae, it was a gilded cage.

He now sat on the wide cushioned bench near the balcony, the city glinting beneath a veil of rain. As he watched the rain pour, a memory surfaced—Sonia laughing on their tiny balcony back in Pittsburgh, her hand outstretched to catch the falling raindrops.

"Look, Tae—look!" she'd called, eyes alight with childlike wonder, her fingers dancing in the rain, her laughter echoing like a bell.

He watched as the lights shimmered across the Han River like stars skimming water.

She would've loved this view.

Tae reached out, letting the rain kiss his fingers, chasing the brief sensation, hoping it might bring her back, if only for a moment.

These days he often caught himself forgetting she was gone.

It kept happening—small, unconscious lapses.

On the flight in, as the plane descended, he'd reached for his phone without thinking: snapping a photo of Seoul from above, the city lights glittering like a jeweled necklace against the dark. His fingers had hovered over her name, ready to

111

send it to her.

Then the realization hit—sudden, sharp, cruel—

that he would never be able to send it.

Never be able to share anything with her *ever* again.

The doorbell rang just as he stubbed out the cigarette, crushing the ember with a twist.

He rose, then padded barefoot across the warm stone floor, glancing at the monitor.

It was Minjae.

A moment later, he opened the door.

Minjae stood at the door, shirt collar loosened, suit jacket draped over one arm. His glasses, slim and stylish, framed his striking features with effortless precision. He held a plastic takeout bag in one hand and two chilled cans in the other.

A familiar scent rose in the air—crispy, savory, unmistakable.

"Kyochon," he said simply. "And some Yebisu Premium to go with it."

He handed Tae the chicken and beer, then stepped inside without waiting for an invitation.

"Figured I'd join you for dinner since you skipped lunch."

Tae raised a brow.

How did he—?

Then he smiled. *Of course, Secretary Choi.*

"Didn't know you liked fried chicken," he said, reaching for a couple of plates and glasses.

Minjae sank onto the couch, loosening his tie with a sigh.

"I don't. But you do. Kyochon—original soy garlic. Picked it up just for you."

Tae let out a quiet laugh.

"You sure about that? Sounds more like something Secretary Choi would do."

Minjae shrugged and laughed. "You could at least pretend I made the effort. I came with the getup and everything."

They laughed, and for a moment, it felt like the weight of years had lifted.

As Tae poured the drinks, Minjae's gaze fell on the gold band glinting on his brother's finger. His expression shifted, and his voice dropped.

"I heard about Sonia... I'm sorry."

Tae kept his eyes on the glasses. "Yeah."

"I'd hoped to meet her in person. Is that why you're back?"

Tae nodded. "It is. But... there's more to it."

He spoke slowly, walking Minjae through everything—

The article. The email. The missing ring.

The video. The whistle. Hana. And the nagging feeling in his gut that this wasn't an accident Someone had brought Sonia to that cliff. And made sure she never left.

Minjae listened without interrupting, his face unreadable, the muscles in his jaw tight.

When Tae finished, silence settled between them.

"*Arasseo*," Minjae said quietly.

(Understood).

"I agree... it is strange. But if the police don't suspect foul play, I'm not sure what you can find."

He paused, then added.

"Still—if you need anything... let me know. I'll do what I can."

Tae hadn't expected that.

Knowing how cautious and pragmatic Minjae was—with the weight of the Chae family's reputation never far from his mind—he'd assumed his brother would brush it off, urge him to let it go and not stir trouble.

He had expected Minjae's usual logic and cold rationality.

But instead, his brother had listened—had even offered help.

"So when are you meeting this lady... Hana? Do you trust her?"

"I'm still waiting to hear back," Tae said.

"Back when everything happened with Mino... she was the only one who believed me. I think I can trust her."

"All right. Just let me know how it goes. But be careful, Taejoon-ah. If you're right—if someone really is behind this—it could get dangerous."

Tae gave a quiet nod.

Minjae leaned back with a sigh.

"By the way, Eomma asked about you again today. I kept my promise and I didn't tell her you're here yet. But I don't know how much longer I can keep this up."

"*Ajik an dwaesseo. Just give me a little more time.*"

(Not yet.)

Minjae gave a small nod.

"*Geurae.*"

(Okay.)

"Oh, by the way, you probably heard... Sera's engaged to Jaeho."

Tae blinked.

"*Mwo? Jinjja?*"

(What? Seriously?)

Sera was the youngest of their uncle's three children—Minjae and Tae's first cousins. After their father passed, their uncle had stepped in like a second father, and the boys had grown close to his kids: Junsu, the eldest; Yerin, the middle child; and Sera, the baby of the family.

But Tae hadn't realized Jaeho was seeing her.

114

Then again, he hadn't stayed in touch.

It was rare, even now, for someone from a chaebol family, especially a daughter, to get serious with an actor or idol. These pairings happened more often when the man came from money and the woman was in entertainment—as was the case with his mother. The other way around? Far less common.

Tae had assumed their uncle, Chae Joonseok—traditional, proud, and deeply aware of appearances—would never go for it. He would've expected protests, pushback, maybe even a quiet arrangement to end things behind closed doors.

"Times are changing," Minjae said, as if reading his thoughts. "You can't control kids or dictate who they marry. Not unless you want to lose them. They're young, but they seem serious. I think Uncle just decided it was better to accept it. Still... I was surprised you didn't know."

"Well, I haven't exactly stayed in touch with anyone these past few years," Tae murmured, then gave a dry smile. "I guess this means Jaeho's dating clause with Glimmer finally expired."

In the idol world, dating clauses were standard fare: iron-clad rules that banned artists from pursuing romantic relationships for five, sometimes even seven, years.

It was all about maintaining the image of an idol: single, desirable, untouchable.

Love, for an idol, wasn't just discouraged—it was forbidden. A liability, a threat to their market value. A breach of contract that could destroy their career overnight.

Minjae glanced over. "I'm only telling you because there's likely going to be a public engagement soon. The families are planning to meet and make a formal announcement."

Tae looked at him, brow raised.

"Word's already been out for a while," Minjae added. *"K-Eye* published photos of them together last month."

Tae let out a soft breath.

Minjae reached into his coat pocket and handed him a phone.

"They even got a shot of you arriving at the airport."

On the screen was a grainy photo: Tae in his hoodie, head dipped low, just about to slide into Minjae's car.

He remembered that moment now from the airport—that faint *click* in the air as he turned his head—that brief sting of being watched.

So, it had been them.

Of course it had.

K-Eye. The infamous gossip tabloid of the Korean entertainment world.

Powerful, relentless, and feared by everyone in the industry. Known for their ruthless exposés and infamous bombshell scoops and revelations. They'd built their reputation on capturing actors and idols at their weakest.

Every April 1st, the industry braced for impact. PR teams barely slept. Careers were made and broken overnight, all from one grainy zoom-lens photo.

Tae knew their game all too well. Years ago, he'd found himself caught squarely in their crosshairs—dragged into a scandal built on half-truths and manipulated texts.

At the time, he'd expected the worst. But in a rare twist, *K-Eye* had done what no one expected—they actually investigated the claims and exposed the truth, proving that the allegations were baseless.

It had been one of the few moments in his career when the press hadn't buried him, but had pulled him back from the brink.

Still, Tae knew better than to think *K-Eye* played favorites.

And if *K-Eye* had already published pics of Sera and Jaeho, then their relationship was well and truly out.

Tae was reaching for the last piece of chicken—his hand halfway there—when something caught his eye.

A small, reddish mark just beneath Minjae's collar.

A hickey?

He paused, brow lifting. "By the way, what about you, Hyung—are you seeing someone?"

Minjae didn't miss a beat.

"*Aniya. Amudo eopseo.*"

(No. There's no one.)

A mischievous grin lit Tae's face.

"*Geureom i geo mwoya?*"

(Then what's this, huh?)

Minjae flushed—his face already tinged from the alcohol, now turned a deeper shade of red. He fumbled with his collar, tugging it higher.

"*Ah, geunyang... mogae mulin geoya,*" he muttered.

(It's nothing... just a mosquito bite.)

Tae looked at him, eyes glinting.

"*Yogi?*" he said, motioning vaguely at the spotless, climate-controlled luxury apartment.

(Here?)

A quiet chuckle slipped out, the corner of his mouth twitching.

Minjae mumbled something under his breath, adjusting his collar again, not meeting his eyes.

Tae didn't press. But he couldn't help the small, knowing smile that lingered at his lips. His straight-laced brother—actually lying about seeing someone.

He never thought he'd live to see the day.

Minjae had never been the type to bend the truth, not even as a kid. Their mother used to joke that if something went wrong in the house, all she had to do was look at Minjae's face—he'd either confess or give the culprit away with a single blink. He was the one everyone trusted to tell the truth, because he never strayed from it.

And in all their years, Tae had never once known him to show interest in anyone—much less date. He was handsome, successful, heir to the empire. There had never been a shortage of women around him. But Minjae had always been distant.

Courteous, but detached.

So for him to be dodging now, fumbling over unconvincing excuses and awkward glances, blushing like a teenager... must mean she was really someone special.

"*Yah, jangnan-iya,*" Tae said, laughing.

(I'm just teasing.)

"*Jinjja—nan joha,*" he added with a smile.

(Really—I'm happy for you.)

Minjae rose and reached for his coat.

"*Geuman ttalgo, eolleun ja.*"

(Cut it out and get some sleep.)

At the door, he paused.

"If anything happens... you know I'm here. Just a few floors up."

Then, with a faint smile, he added,

"I know—you're all grown up. *Geuraedo neon yeongwonhi nae dongsaeng-iya.*"

(But you'll always be my little brother.)

Tae smiled and nodded as Minjae walked past, tousling his hair with a familiar, brotherly touch.

When the door clicked shut, the silence folded around him

again.

Tae checked his phone.

Two new messages from Hana.

"Naeil bowa."

(Let's meet tomorrow.)

"Na aneun ilbonshikjip isseo."

(There's a Japanese place I know.)

.

Chapter 11

T HE CITY SLID BY as lights streaked across the car windows like brushstrokes.

Tae leaned against the window, his forehead grazing the cool, tinted glass, watching Seoul blur into motion.

LED billboards blazed above sleek department stores, their displays shifting from dewy-skinned skincare models to idol group teasers in a flash. A motorbike zipped between lanes, a red delivery box strapped to the back, just as a mother clutched her son's hand and hurried across the street. Along the sidewalks, couples strolled hand in hand—some in matching windbreakers, others pausing for selfies beneath the neon lights.

As they paused at a red light, Tae saw signs in Hangul stacked over cafés, karaoke rooms, clinics, and *pojangmachas*—small tented street stalls glowing orange like lanterns in the dusk.

Inside one, people huddled on plastic stools, hunched over steaming bowls. Pots of *tteokbokki* bubbled in thick red sauce, *odeng* skewers soaked in golden broth, and plates of *soondae* sizzled on portable burners. A middle-aged man in a padded jacket raised a shot of soju in a quiet toast with his friends, while an older woman ladled broth into paper cups with practiced ease.

He checked the time—they were running late.

He should've taken the subway.

The Seoul Metro was famously efficient, and—strangely—the commute always calmed him.

The quiet shuffle of fellow commuters, the steady ebb and flow of bodies moving in sync. A soft chime and a polite measured voice announcing each stop—*"Seongsu-yeok, imnida"* (This is Seongsu Station)—followed by the familiar thud of doors sliding shut and the gentle jolt of departure.

As a student, he had to beg his mother to let him take the subway alone. Perhaps it had been loneliness, a desire to be around people—even strangers.

Later, as Orion rose to fame, public transit grew trickier.

But a mask, a cap and a hoodie usually did the trick. If he kept his head down and his hoodie up, no one looked twice. For those fleeting rides, he wasn't Park Taejoon the idol—just another face in the crowd.

But Minjae had intervened.

"Just let Secretary Choi drive you," he'd said, his tone calm but firm. "There's no need to wander around alone right now."

So thanks to his brother, here he was, inching through traffic toward the tiny Japanese restaurant Hana had chosen in Apgujeong. What could've been a twenty-minute subway ride had already stretched past forty.

Now the city began to shift. The sleek towers of Gangnam receded in the rearview mirror, replaced by the quieter charm of Samcheong-dong, a neighborhood where time seemed to slow.

The streets narrowed. Walls of worn brick were laced with ivy, and traditional hanok rooftops curved against the skyline. Even the air felt different here: quieter, more hushed.

The car eased to a stop in front of a low wooden building with a narrow doorway.

A pair of *noren* curtains, narrow fabric panels traditionally hung over doorways in Japanese shops, fluttered lightly in the breeze, marked with the kanji: *momono hana* or peach blossom. There was no flashy neon sign, no sidewalk menu. Just a discreet entrance tucked in the stone walls. The kind of place only locals knew.

Secretary Choi pulled up and cut the engine.

Tae exhaled slowly as he ran a hand through his hair, and reached for the door.

It was time to meet her.

* * *

Inside, the restaurant was warm and spare.

Pale wooden walls framed the place, warm lanterns cast a muted glow, along with the faint sound of a stream trickling from a bamboo water feature running somewhere behind the paper screen walls.

Diners sat cross-legged at low tables—around nine tables in total—shoes removed and tucked neatly on wooden shelves near the entrance. The air was rich with the scent of dashi, miso and grilled saba fish.

Soft murmurs rose and fell, punctuated by the occasional clink of porcelain and the quiet shuffle of servers in muted gray uniforms.

Tae spotted Hana at a table in the back alcove.

She sat alone, her dark green blazer folded neatly over the

chair beside her. Her phone lay screen-down next to a pristine ceramic teacup. Her eyes were locked in concentration on the items in front of her, hands moving with quiet precision.

She gently aligned the chopsticks until they lay perfectly parallel, then shifted the dipping dishes into symmetry, angling the soy sauce dish just so. Finally she adjusted her spoon by a millimeter and straightened the edge of a napkin with care.

Tae slipped off his shoes, murmured a polite *"Annyeong-haseyo"* to the hostess, and walked across the tatami mat toward her.

She glanced up as he approached, and their eyes met.

She looked just the way he remembered—composed, quietly striking in that way that never asked for attention, but somehow held it anyway. Her hair was loosely tied back, her makeup soft, barely there. There was a steadiness in the way she sat, in the set of her shoulders, the calm clarity in her brown eyes.

He'd forgotten how warm her gaze could be—how it didn't just look at you but seemed to see through you. And for a moment, he found himself holding it longer than he meant to.

"Yeojeonhi gatda," he said softly, a faint smile tugging at his lips.

(You haven't changed.)

Hana's eyes flickered, but her expression remained steady.

"Neoneun jogeum dalla."

(You look a little different.)

"Ajikdo jalsaenggyeotne," she said with a small shrug.

(Still handsome, though.)

"Kind of unfair, honestly," she added.

Tae let out a small laugh at her bluntness and lowered himself onto the cushion across from her.

123

"*Oraenmaniya,*" he said.

(It's been a while.)

"*Daeche eolmana dwaetji?*" she nodded.

(How long has it been?)

"*O nyen jeongdo?*"

(Maybe five years?)

A server appeared, bowing as he poured steaming cups of barley tea before retreating.

Tae took a sip, then glanced down.

Everything on their table looked meticulously arranged—chopsticks, dipping bowls, spoons arranged perfectly, nothing even slightly out of place.

And yet, as he watched, Hana re-adjusted one of the dishes by a hair, her fingers steady and deliberate, moving with near-clinical precision.

He tilted his head slightly.

"Do you always do this?"

Hana looked up, mid-adjustment, pausing for half a beat before giving a light shrug.

"It helps me think," she said simply.

Tae nodded, a flicker of surprise crossing his face. He hadn't remembered this about her.

Then again, they hadn't known each other all that well.

"So," Hana said, folding her hands. "What have you been up to? I don't see you on screens anymore."

"I'm a PhD student now. Completing my degree in the US. Left the industry. Planning to be a professor."

"*Jeongmal?*" she said, raising an eyebrow.

(Really?)

He gave her a faint smile.

"*Keurigo neo?*"

124

(And you?)

"Retired from the force," she said. "I do PI work now. Smaller stuff—civil, domestic cases mainly—cheating spouses, background checks. Nothing major."

He nodded again, slowly this time.

"So, I guess we both left our old lives behind."

But even as he said it, a quiet question tugged at him.

Hana had been the best detective he'd known. When they met, she'd been on the fast track to promotion. She'd loved the work and took pride in it.

So what had changed?

"You were really good at it," he said quietly. "Police work. You had a way of seeing things that others missed. And you genuinely cared about people and went out of your way to help them. I always found that admirable."

Hana didn't respond right away. Her gaze drifted down to her tea.

"Yeah... well," she said eventually. "Sometimes that can cost you more than you're willing to pay."

Then she glanced back at him.

"But *you*—a professor?"

A small smile played at the corners of her mouth.

"How does one go from idol to professor? How does that even happen? That's some next-level plot twist."

Tae chuckled. "I guess it sounds strange. But I was always academically inclined. My dad and hyung both went to business schools in the States. And believe it or not, I actually graduated at the top of my class in Business. So, a PhD in Management made sense."

"*Jinjja?*" Hana looked genuinely surprised.

(Seriously?)

125

Then she tilted her head, giving him a half-smile.

"I guess I shouldn't be too surprised. You're a *Chae*, after all. Business runs in your blood."

"Wait—how did you know that?"

"It's my job to know," she said, her tone even, matter-of-fact. "I figured it out five years back when we met. It wasn't public knowledge, but it wasn't too hard to piece together—especially once I learned who your mother was."

Tae blinked for a second, momentarily caught off guard.

"I guess I shouldn't be surprised," he said, rubbing the back of his neck.

He paused, then continued. "Anyway... back in undergrad, a few of my business professors encouraged me to get into research. I liked it. I just never had the chance to continue. Everything got swallowed up by idol life—schedules, appearances, tours, endorsements. There was barely time to breathe, let alone study."

"So, when I finally left the industry, I decided to go back to the one thing I always enjoyed but never got to do."

Hana studied him for a moment, her expression unreadable. Then she nodded.

"*Geugeo jinjja mal duinae.*"

(Now that I think about it, that actually makes sense.)

Tae met her eyes.

"*Geurae?*"

(Does it?)

"Eung," she said softly. "*Seonsaengnim-i jal eoullyeo.*"

(Yeah. Being a professor suits you.)

A warm smile touched his lips.

It was the first time someone had said that to him.

Most people just blinked in disbelief when he told them. But he could tell, she meant it.

For a moment, they sat in comfortable stillness.

Then Hana leaned back slightly, arms folding across her chest.

"So... why reach out now?" she asked getting straight to the point.

Tae reached into his coat pocket and pulled out his phone.

"Her name is Sonia. She is—*was*—my fiancé."

Something shifted in Hana's eyes.

"Oh," she said gently. "I'm sorry."

She glanced at the screen, brows furrowing.

"I think I saw something in the news about her. Jeju, right? Accidental fall while taking a photo?"

He nodded.

"That's what they said—except it wasn't an accident. I don't believe that for a second."

He tapped his phone and brought up a video.

Sonia's face appeared on the screen.

Tae handed it to Hana.

"She sent me this a few days back. And there are things that don't add up."

Tae exhaled, then continued.

"She was uncomfortable with heights. She didn't know anyone in Jeju. She'd never even been to Korea. Then there's her phone; it was found intact next to her. Why didn't it break when she fell from that height? Also, the engagement ring I gave her is missing. Everything else was there. Why just that?"

Hana watched the video in silence.

When it ended, she set the phone down with care.

"Tae... if the police ruled it accidental, there's not much anyone can do. I've been down that road. You run into walls—

doors that won't open."

"I know. Minjae said something similar. But I know this wasn't an accident. And you're the only one I trust."

He paused.

"I am going to Jeju. I want you to come with me... help me find out what *really* happened."

"Listen," she said, hesitating, her tone measured. "I don't take on cases like this anymore. That kind of work... it costs too much. It took me a long time to get over the past and start fresh. I'm done with all that."

"But—"

"*Biane*," she said softly, starting to rise.

(Sorry.)

Tae looked up at her.

"What happened to the detective who wouldn't stop until she found the truth? Who believed in justice and helping victims even when no one else did? Who believed in me when no one else would?"

Hana froze for a second, then met his eyes.

"She... *died*."

He saw it then—the hurt beneath her words.

A heaviness that hadn't been there five years ago.

The shadow of something unspoken.

A server returned, setting down two small bowls of *chawanmushi*, a light savory Japanese egg custard.

Neither of them reached for their spoons.

Hana stood fully now, slipping into her coat.

"It was nice to see you, Tae," she said, her voice low but firm.

"And if I'm being honest... I'd drop this if I were you. I'm sorry I couldn't help."

She gave him one last look, then turned and walked out.

She didn't look back.

* * *

The clock on the nightstand glowed.

1:03 a.m.

Tae lay in bed, eyes locked on the ceiling.

Shadows danced above him, thin and jagged, scattering with every car that passed by outside.

Sleep refused to come.

His mind replayed the conversation with Hana.

He hadn't expected her to say no—watching her walk away had hurt more than he was willing to admit.

He had come all the way here, convinced she would help. She'd been the one person he was sure would believe him.

In fact, he had been so sure that she'd help, that he hadn't thought of a plan B.

Now, he didn't know what to do anymore.

His eyes drifted to his suitcase by the closet, still unpacked.

From the corner of the bed, he could just make out a small shape peeking out: the brown, rounded foot of a teddy bear.

He hadn't taken it out since arriving. Couldn't bring himself to.

He reached for his phone and opened his gallery.

There were hundreds of images and videos—of Sonia and him.

Five years of beautiful memories, still bright and intact.

He smiled as they scrolled by with the swipe of his finger.

There she was in the kitchen, holding a ladle like a mic, singing off-key in flannel pajamas. Another showed her flopped on the floor in defeat, surrounded by a sea of rejected outfits before her cousin's wedding.

He tapped a video: Sonia with chopsticks stuck in her hair, cheeks puffed.

"Tae-tae," she said, her voice echoing through the phone as she grinned into the lens, "you're gonna love this look. It's space princess meets kitchen warrior."

Her voice played in his head, clear as day—goofy, radiant... untouchable.

His thumb hovered over her final video.

Hesitated.

Then tapped.

He placed the phone on the nightstand and slipped in his AirPods.

The screen glowed softly beside him as her voice played— warm, soft, familiar.

He closed his eyes, picturing her smiling as she spoke.

His heart always waited for the same line.

The one where she said, "I love you."

That's when he would whisper, "I love you too."

And let himself drift.

This had become his nightly ritual.

But tonight just as he turned slightly in bed, his shoulder pressed against the phone—and the volume jumped.

He reached to adjust it.

That's when he heard it—

A faint tune.

A low whistle.

Tae's eyes flew open.

He bolted upright, heart thudding in his chest.

He grabbed the phone, scrubbing back through the timeline, increasing the volume.

There—there it was again.

That same sound. The whistle.

Barely audible—but unmistakable.

His breath caught. His thumb dragged along the frame bar.

He rewound. Slowed the playback. Frame by frame.

Sonia was smiling.

Twirling the camera.

Talking to him.

But then—

Timestamp 00:24.6

He paused just as she turned.

Just for a breath, less than a second, he watched as her gaze shifted—

Not toward the camera.

Not toward him.

But off to the side.

And then as he replayed in slow-motion, he saw her smile.

Like she was sharing a secret… with someone.

Someone present—who was watching her from the corner.

It was fleeting.

Just a few seconds.

The kind of thing you'd never notice unless you knew where to look.

But now that he saw it, he *knew*.

Someone had been with her that day. At that cliff.

Not a stranger in the distance. Someone close.

Someone she recognized.

Someone she had trusted.

That same whistle.

The one he had heard the night Mino died.

He felt chills down his spine as his blood went cold.

His heart pounded against his ribs, erratic and wild.
He grabbed his phone and opened a message thread.

> **[Sent Video]**
> *This wasn't an accident.*
> *I heard it. The whistle.*
> *Same as before.*
> *Whoever killed Mino... they were there with Sonia.*
> *You have to help me.*

He stared at the screen, barely breathing.

> **Read.**
> Three dots appeared.
> *Hana is typing…*
> Then—
> **Hana:**
> *I'll get the sound analyzed.*
> A pause.
> And then—
> **Hana:**
> *When's that flight to Jeju?*

Tae exhaled, body trembling, relieved, hopeful.

He knew she was in.

He leaned back against the pillows, heart still hammering in his chest, skin damp with cold sweat.

The room was quiet—but it didn't feel still.

There was a tension in the dark. A weight.

That crawling sensation of being watched, even though he knew he was alone.

And then, the sound played—not from the video, not from his phone—but inside his mind.

That whistle, looped again and again, faint but insistent.

A cheerful tune.

A lullaby?

He had heard it before. He was sure of it.

Long before Mino. Before Sonia.

But where? Why couldn't he place it?

The melody coiled at the edge of his mind like smoke—elusive, taunting, refusing to be named.

And yet, he knew.

This wasn't random. None of this was: Mino's death, then Sonia's. It had something to do with *him*. With the past.

His own lips parted, almost unconsciously, and he began to whistle in the pitch dark.

Slowly, carefully, trying to mimic the rise and fall of that tune.

Note by note.

The haunting melody filled the room.

And then—

A second after he stopped—

he thought he heard something.

From somewhere beyond the walls,

or maybe from the frayed edges of memory itself,

came the distant echo of…

children's laughter.

Chapter 12

NARI HUMMED UNDER her breath as she sat cross-legged on the floor, carefully shading in the roof of a house with her red crayon.

From the television, a bright jingle floated through the apartment—*"Eomma Dalmatne"*—that cheerful, singsong lullaby every Korean child knew by heart.

On-screen, a chorus of animated children clapped and swayed, their high-pitched voices singing in sync. The cartoon Dalmatian danced in circles, floppy ears bouncing, as the sounds of children's laughter bubbled between verses.

Nari moved her lips in time with the lyrics, silently mouthing each word, letting the cartoon do the singing for her.

Nun-do dalmatne
  (Your eyes look the same)
  Ko-do dalmatne
  (Your nose looks the same)
  Ip-do dalmatne
  (Your lips look the same)
  Eomma dalmatne
  (You look like your mom)
  Uri eomma yeppeujiyo

(Our mom is pretty, right?)
Nado yeppeujiyo
(I'm pretty too, right?)
Uri eomma dalmatseoyo
(I look just like my mom)
Jeongmal dalmatne
(Really look like her!)

Beside her, Eomma sat cross-legged on a worn floor cushion, methodically rinsing rice in a metal bowl.

In the other room, Abeoji rustled his newspaper, occasionally clicking his tongue at the headlines.

Then came a knock—sharp, abrupt, unexpected—shattering the momentary peace.

A sudden, brutal thud against the door, rattling the apartment like a thunderclap. It was the kind of sound that didn't wait for permission.

It was followed by three rapid and sharp strikes—clean and precise—that reverberated through the thin walls like warning shots.

Nari froze.

She knew the rhythm of that knock.

Sharp. Impatient. Like the back of a hand demanding obedience.

Eomma did too.

She stood at once, the bowl of rice tipping slightly, water sloshing onto the floor. Her hand reached for Nari without hesitation, guiding her toward the tiny closet beside the sink—the one just big enough for a child to disappear.

She crouched, brushed a strand of hair from Nari's face, and looked her square in the eye.

135

"Don't come out, no matter what," she whispered.

But she didn't need to say it.

Nari had already seen the signs—the hard line of her mother's mouth, the tremor in her hands, the familiar sheen of panic beginning to glisten along her brow.

She crawled into the dark, holding her breath as the door shut quietly behind her, leaving only a sliver for her to see through.

The happy song kept playing.

Inside the closet, Nari curled in on herself, folding her body so small she could disappear, wedged between coats that smelled faintly of mothballs and old fabric softener. A loose thread brushed against her cheek, but she didn't move. Instead she pulled her knees up tighter to her chest.

The narrow shaft of sunlight that had crept through the crack in the closet door was now gone, replaced by the shadow of fear.

She held her breath.

Her heart thudded, each beat a small betrayal. She feared the sound might give her away, feared that even her thoughts were too loud.

The apartment was deathly still.

The faucet stopped running. Even the faint hum of the refrigerator quieted, as though the room itself had drawn in a breath and refused to let it go.

Only the TV continued playing, oblivious to its surroundings, until its happy jingle trailed off into silence as Eomma reached out, her hand trembling, and switched it off.

Another knock.

This one sharper. Measured. Not a request.

Eomma flinched—elbow locking mid-motion—her hands

suspended above the bowl of soaking rice. The water shimmered, unsettled.

Abeoji was still as he sat hunched over the low table. The paper lay open, but he was no longer. His fingers twitched.

Slowly he stood.

His face was pale, lips dry. He looked thinner than even a month ago. His sweater hung at the shoulders, cuffs unraveled like tattered rope. The holes in his sleeves had gotten larger, and his trousers sagged on his hips.

The man who had once stormed through the apartment like thunder now looked like a ghost barely holding shape, as though a gust of wind might carry him away.

Then came the voice.

"Yah! Park Dong-seok! Ne gibang an inneun geo da anda!"

(Park Dong-seok! We know you're in there!)

The voices outside were familiar to Nari.

She had heard them before.

They had come here before.

Abeoji's hand clutched the edge of the newspaper, hoping it could anchor him, as the blood drained from his fingertips.

"We're being patient, *ahjussi!*" one of them called out, the word *ahjussi*—mister—laced with mock respect that only sharpened the threat beneath.

"Don't make us regret it."

It wasn't just one man.

There were at least three.

Their tones were casual but sharp—that sing-song menace particular to men who'd grown used to fear.

Abeoji stood and ran a hand through his hair. He looked at Eomma and muttered, "Stay quiet. Don't say anything."

Eomma stared back, unmoving.

"You promised me they wouldn't come here again," she whispered.

"Just go inside. Pretend we're not home."

"They know we're here."

The next knock wasn't a knock—it was a blow.

Someone had kicked the door, sending it shuddering in its frame.

Nari's heartbeat surged in her ears, a frantic rhythm rising with every thud—pounding so fast it felt as though it might tear through her chest.

"Geunyang yeoreo!"

(Just open up!)

"Eojjeol geoya?"

(You think this is going to stop us?)

Then came a quieter voice, softer and more dangerous in its calm, slick with false civility.

"Hyungnim has been very patient."

From the narrow crack in the closet door, Nari could see Abeoji's face turn to a shade of ash. He shuffled toward the door, as though gravity had grown heavier. But not before glancing toward the bedroom, where Eomma had already disappeared.

His shoulders were hunched, spine bent, a show of defeat.

Then, slowly, he unlatched the door.

It creaked open.

Three men stepped in.

Two of them were dressed in padded jackets, the kind worn by ordinary deliverymen, like they belonged to the city. But it was clear that there was nothing ordinary about them.

The first man, tall and trim in a camel-colored coat, was impeccably dressed: hair slicked back, his coat cinched at the waist like a businessman on his way to a meeting. He had a disarming smile and moved with the confidence of someone who knew he'd already won.

His cologne was strong—Nari could smell it even from the next room—a strange mix of peppermint and smoke, crisp but bitter. His eyes glinted, though his smile stayed soft: danger disguised as courtesy.

The second was shorter but broader, a heavyset man in a black bomber jacket. His fist wrapped around a steel baton he didn't bother to hide. He looked bored, like he'd done this a hundred times.

The third was younger, restless, in a track suit and beanie. He was chewing gum with the kind of loud arrogance of a schoolboy who kicked lockers just to watch someone flinch.

"*Aigoo,*" the tall one drawled, his tone steeped with mock sympathy as he surveyed the cramped apartment like a landlord inspecting a soon-to-be eviction.

"Still the same place, Hyung? You haven't even tried to upgrade?"

Abeoji bowed slightly.

"Please. We have a child. I lost my job. We're trying to make ends meet."

The man didn't even look at him.

His gaze wandered across the room.

"It smells in here," he muttered, scrunching his nose with feigned delicacy.

He stepped farther in, inspecting the cramped space. His eyes landed on the rice cooker, the electric fan missing a blade, the discolored wallpaper curling at the corners.

From the closet, Nari saw her father bowing again and again. She heard the slight hitch in his voice as he begged:

139

"Please. I just need a little more time. I—I'm trying. I—I have a lead. They said they might call this week."

The man in the bomber jacket snorted.

"He said that last month. And the month before."

The tall man wandered the room with slow deliberation, poking at corners with his shoe, flipping a spoon off the counter.

"Hyungnim doesn't like broken promises," he said, non-nonchalantly

One of the men tugged open the fridge door and laughed

"No food in the fridge. You feed your kid with what?" he asked, pulling open drawers, cabinets, his voice thick with mock concern. "Prayers?"

"Nothing here but old gochujang and baking soda," said the man with the baton.

"Maybe that's what she eats," the bomber jacket man smirked. "Builds character."

Nari's breath slowed to a hush. Her fingers curled around her knees. Through the slats, she could make out Abeoji—still bowing, again and again.

His voice had begun to crack.

"Please. I swear, I'll pay. We're going through a really hard time. As you can see, I don't even have enough to buy food."

The gum-chewing one chuckled. "Hey, if you can't pay up, at least don't insult us with your sob stories."

Drawers slammed. Cabinets opened. One of them hummed softly, almost cheerfully, as he swept things off the shelf.

The tall one crouched slightly, inspecting Abeoji as if he were a broken machine.

"You think Hyungnim is a monster? He's not. He under-stands hardship. You make your payments, and he leaves you alone. Simple."

He leaned down, getting close to Abeoji's face.

"We don't enjoy this, Hyung. We really don't. But you're three months behind. Hyungnim's patience isn't infinite."

Then he straightened and walked over to the TV.

He looked and found a pair of Eomma's earrings on the table. Picked them up. "Cute."

He pocketed them.

"No, please..." Abeoji started to say, but stopped.

He knew better.

Eomma appeared then, her voice steady.

"We have nothing. Take this month's payment and leave."

She extended a thin envelope.

Slick Hair took it, counted quickly, and tsked.

"Not even half."

"That's all we have."

The baton in the other man's hand twitched.

Slick Hair turned toward Abeoji.

"Then we'll take something else, hm?"

He nodded once.

The baton swung down—not on them, but the rice cooker.

CRACK.

Nari jumped inside the closet.

Then the younger one made a sound.

"Yo. What's this?"

He let out a low whistle and pulled something from beneath the altar cabinet. It was Eomma's cedar box.

"Put that down," Eomma said.

Her voice was quiet but firm.

"Please. That box... that's all I have."

The man in the bomber jacket turned to her.

"Lady, you think we care about your stupid box?"

He snatched it out of the younger man's hand.

Opened it.

A jade necklace glinted under the bare ceiling bulb.

Deep green as sea glass.

Simple. Beautiful.

"Real jade?" the tall one mused, holding it up to the light. "Nice. Looks like something worth keeping."

Eomma stepped forward.

"It belonged to my mother," she said. "It's for my daughter. For when she grows up."

The man smiled faintly, as if amused by the sentiment.

Then, slowly, he slipped the necklace into his coat pocket.

"Too bad," he said.

Then he threw the box on the ground.

It shattered against the floor.

Eomma sank to her knees, eyes locked on the broken wood and velvet.

She didn't make a sound. Just stared.

Nari felt something inside her tighten.

"Please," Eomma whispered, standing again, blocking their path. "That necklace is for my daughter. It's all I can give her."

The tall one's expression didn't shift, but his voice chilled.

"Then maybe you should teach your husband to honor his debts."

He leaned closer to her. Too close.

"Or maybe next time, Hyungnim will ask for something more... personal."

Abeoji launched himself forward.

A flash of motion—and then a crash.

He was thrown back easily.

The baton man shoved him, hard, slamming him back against the wall. Abeoji slid down like paper, coughing, legs folding beneath him.

The noise in Nari's ears grew loud. Like crashing waves. Her small fists clenched around her knees. She wanted to scream but knew she couldn't.

Finally, the men moved to leave.

Before going, the tall man straightened his coat, turned and said: "Next week. Final. No more delays. Or next time, we come with scissors."

He tapped his fingers together, miming a snip.

They left.

The door slammed.

For a long time, no one moved.

Abeoji was still crumpled against the wall, head buried in his hands. His shoulders trembled.

Eomma knelt beside the shattered cedar box, her back straight, body unmoving. Her eyes were vacant, staring through the shards as though trying to will time backward.

Her lips parted, dry and soundless at first.

Then, finally, she spoke—not to anyone, not even to herself. Just into the air.

"They took it... I saved it for Nari. Her necklace. They took it. They took her necklace."

Usually, Abeoji would have snapped at her for that. Told her to shut up. Called her names.

But not today.

He rose on unsteady legs, as if pulled by something heavier than his own will. Without a word, he wrapped his arms around Eomma and held her.

From the closet, Nari heard his breath falter.

Then, came a sound—low and fractured—like something inside him broke.

He began to cry.

Not in shouts or curses, but in quiet, broken sobs.

He wept the way a man does when he has nothing left to offer.

A hollowed-out cry from the pit of the soul.

And then—so did Eomma.

Soft, hopeless weeps that filled the apartment more loudly than any shouts ever could. Wordless grief echoing between the walls.

In the dark, Nari sat curled into herself. Her small fingers clutched her ankles. Her throat prickled. Her eyes burned. But the tears wouldn't come.

***

Later that night, she watched from the shadowed hallway as Abeoji sat beside Eomma, a spoon in one hand and a small bottle in the other.

His movements were slow, careful—like he feared that any sudden gesture might undo her completely.

Eomma shook her head, her voice barely a whisper.

"I don't want to take that… it makes me feel strange."

Abeoji didn't argue, didn't raise his voice like he would have.

He simply murmured, "It's good for you. You must take it."

There was no tension in the room. No shouting. No edge to his words.

Just a quiet, unfamiliar tenderness, that felt so out of place it made the air feel heavier.

Something had changed between them.

Then Abeoji looked up and saw Nari.

And for the first time in a long time, he acknowledged her.

A gentle smile played on his face—small, almost shy.

It was meant to comfort.

But instead... it unsettled her.

Chapter 13

THE DAY WAS ACHINGLY beautiful.

The sky stretched overhead in a vault of pale, crystalline blue, already beginning to burn crimson near the horizon. The sun hovered low, casting its final light, spilling like honey across the rugged cliffs of Seopjikoji, a remote and windswept point on the far eastern edge of Jeju Island.

All around the raw beauty of Jeju unfolded: wind-twisted black pines, fields of wild grass tinged with gold, bowing to the sea breeze. Distant *haenyeo* statues—stoic stone figures honoring the island's legendary female divers who once braved the ocean's depths—stood watch over the coast like guardians of the sea.

Jeju in the off-season was quiet, almost sacred.

Tae stood alone at the top of the cliff. The wind rolled in from the ocean, cool and saline, threading through the landscape. It wound around Tae as if it recognized him, curling against the edges of his coat, tugging at his hair with gentle insistence, as though trying to lure him forward—towards the edge.

It was the exact spot that had claimed Sonia's life.

Beneath him lay the vast and majestic South Sea.

Its waters were a kaleidoscope of color—a living palette of deep sapphire, jade, cobalt and dark emerald—shifting with the light, foaming with white-capped waves that hurled themselves again and again against the ancient black volcanic rocks.

The air was rich with the scent of brine, wet stone and kelp, and the faint sweetness of pine carried in from the groves farther inland.

Tae stepped closer to the brink and peered over the edge.

The drop was steep—harrowing.

The cliff fell away violently beneath his boots.

Far below, the black jagged rocks looked like broken teeth—sharp, wet, glistening and waiting… like open jaws.

It was the kind of fall that offered no mercy.

No second chances.

He imagined Sonia standing where he stood now.

His fists clenched.

What had she felt?

Did she know what was coming in those final seconds?

He closed his eyes as a twist of nausea curled in his stomach.

And then, out of nowhere—

A whistle.

Low. Familiar. Dissonant.

It came from behind.

Tae froze.

The warmth from the sunlight drained as the melody slid into his ears like a secret—

Coiled, quiet, intimate.

He turned, eyes wide, heart pounding—

Nothing.

Just the grass swaying, rustling like whispers across the

windswept cliffs.

Then—

Suddenly.

Two hands.

Crept up behind him.

And shoved—sudden, brutal.

No warning.

Tae lurched forward.

The cliff disappeared beneath him.

The ground—the only thing that had ever made sense—was *gone*.

The air split open, shrieking past his ears.

His stomach dropped.

His legs kicked, arms flailed—

as he grasped for air, for rock, for something.

Anything.

The sea surged toward him.

The black rocks rose below—

Sharp, wet, waiting...

He tumbled, flipped.

His spine arched, throat burned.

He tried to scream.

But it was crushed by the howling wind.

Salt scorched his nose.

His eyes stung with wind and terror.

Everything blurred.

The knowing hit—

I'm going to die.

Here. Now.

The last thing he felt was fear.

Raw. Primal.

Screaming inside him.

In every cell.

I don't want to die.

And then he felt—

A touch.

Gentle. Steady.

On his shoulder.

Tae staggered back—

yanked from the edge by his name,

Sharp and clear,

slicing through the haze.

"TAE!"

His mind jerked back into the present.

He blinked and gasped.

He was standing at the cliff's edge—dangerously close.

One more step and there would be no coming back.

His breath came in short bursts, as he heard his heart hammering against his ribs, like a drum.

Detective Yoon Hana stood beside him, her hand still resting gently on his shoulder. Her windbreaker flapped in the strong breeze. Her expression was composed, but her eyes were searching his with a calm intensity, filled with concern.

"Tae…" she said again, her voice low and grounding.

"*Gwaenchanha?*"

(Are you okay?)

He drew a sharp breath, clutching his chest as if to reassure himself that his heart was still beating.

"I—" he started, then faltered.

He exhaled, shaky.

"*Biane.*"

(Sorry.)

149

"I didn't mean to scare you. I was just... standing here, imagining. What she went through. Knowing she... was about to—"

His voice faltered.

The rest wouldn't come.

He turned his gaze back to the sea, to the waves still breaking—relentless, without pause or mercy.

"I need to find them," he said quietly.

"Whoever did this. I don't care what it takes. I'll find them."

Hana nodded solemnly.

"I spoke to the local precinct," she said. "They didn't find anything new. No footage. No signs of another person with her. No confirmed witnesses."

Hana paused for a second, a shadow of doubt crossing her face.

Tae caught the shift in her expression.

"Museun saenggakhae?"

(What are you thinking?)

"Just that... you said Sonia didn't speak Korean, and this was her first time in Korea, right?"

He nodded. *"Geurae."*

(That's right.)

"Then why come all the way out here?" Hana asked.

"This stretch of Seopjikoji is remote. No foot traffic. No tourist facilities. If she wanted to record a birthday video for you, why not go to Seongsan Ilchulbong? It's scenic, popular and safe. It just doesn't make sense why she'd choose a secluded cliffside no one visits."

Tae's lips pressed into a hard line.

Seongsan Ilchulbong—"Sunrise Peak"—was a UNESCO World Heritage Site and the most-visited location on the island.

"*Nado dong-uihae,*" he said.

(I agree.)

"I don't see her coming here on her own."

Hana nodded. "Then, I guess let's check out the guesthouse."

"Maybe someone there saw something that could help us."

***

The drive to the guesthouse the next morning was quiet.

They passed through sleepy roads flanked by black stone walls, low and moss-covered, carved from cooled lava. On either side, rows of *hallabong*—Jeju's famously sweet, bulbous-topped tangerines—glistened under the morning sun.

Stalls selling fresh *hallabong* juice popped up every few kilometers, their faded umbrellas fluttering in the breeze. Wooden signposts in Hangul and English pointed toward coastal temples, equestrian farms, and lava tube caves.

To the east, the sea shimmered, gentle now, with fishing boats drifting like ink strokes on canvas. The sky was postcard-blue, punctuated by slow-turning white wind turbines.

Banners advertising horseback rides and fresh seafood flapped gently above old buildings and open-air markets.

They arrived at the guesthouse, hidden behind a grove of tall cedar trees, just beyond the bend of the coastal trail—where the beaten path gave way to a narrow gravel road.

It was a modest looking place, known as Haebit House or "House of Sunlight." There was a quaint, almost storybook charm about the place with its cream-painted walls, scalloped awnings, wood-paneled balconies, potted succulents, and an old stone pathway leading to the main entrance.

The house itself was low and square, built in the traditional Jeju style with dark basalt stone and a thatched tile roof, the kind once used by farmers and fishermen. A faint trail of pine smoke drifted from a flue at the back, carrying the scent of burning wood.

It was the kind of place most tourists overlooked—built for quiet escapes and solitude.

There were no eye-catching signs, no glossy banners offering panoramic views or breakfast sets. Just a hand-carved wooden placard nailed to a weathered gate, the name etched in Hangul and English beneath a faded motif of a sun cresting the sea.

Inside, a bespectacled man at the front desk bowed politely when they entered.

"We have an appointment with Mr. Baek," Hana said, her tone calm but firm.

The man nodded without a word and quietly stepped away to summon the owner.

The guesthouse had only nine rooms. It was run by an elderly couple, Mr. and Mrs. Baek, who had lived on the island their entire lives.

Moments later, Mr. Baek appeared—a broad-shouldered man in his early seventies—with a build of a former athlete and silver-streaks in his thick hair. He led them into a modest office. The smell of barley tea lingered in the air.

His voice was formal, his expression carefully neutral.

"We already gave our statement to the police," he said, his tone polite but guarded.

Hana stepped forward and gave a slight bow.

"I understand. I'm Hana Seo, former detective with the Seoul Metropolitan Police. We're conducting a private investigation."

She held out her business card with both hands, head inclined.

Mr. Baek accepted it with the same formality, gave it a brief glance, then tucked it away with a small nod.

His expression remained neutral.

Then Hana gestured to Tae.

"And this is Mr. Park. He's here on behalf of the Chae family."

Recognition dawned in Mr. Baek's eyes, and his demeanor shifted instantly. His posture straightened, more formal now. He bowed, more fully this time.

Tae spoke quietly. "Sonia Moore—the guest who passed away—was my fiancée."

"Jinsim-euro choui deurimnida," Mr. Baek said.

(My deepest condolences.)

"We had no idea she was connected to such a prominent family. Please—whatever you need, we'll assist however we can."

"We're just trying to understand what happened," Hana said gently.

Mr. Baek nodded solemnly.

"Of course," he said, folding his hands in front of him.

"As far as we know, Ms. Moore arrived here alone. She stayed with us in suite 4B. Two suitcases. Everything was prepaid. There were no registered visitors. When she didn't check out and her luggage remained untouched for more than a day, we tried calling the number listed on her reservation. But there was no answer. When another day passed and the luggage was still in the room, we reported it to the authorities."

"Any outgoing calls from her room? Or signs she was meeting someone?" Hana asked. "Perhaps you have some surveillance footage we could review?"

Mr. Baek shook his head. "I'm afraid not."

"We're a small family-run establishment. We've never had cause to install CCTV."

He turned and called over a young woman from reception.

She approached quietly, a hint of nervousness in her step. She looked to be in her twenties, with peach-colored hair framing a round, bright face. Her name tag read: Jiwon.

When Mr. Baek asked her about Sonia, Jiwon nodded.

"Geunyeoreul gieokhamnida."

(I remember her.)

"She was polite. Soft-spoken. Smiled a lot. I checked her in that afternoon. After that… I'm not sure. I left before dinner. I didn't see her again after my shift ended. I'm sorry."

She hesitated, shifting slightly. Then her eyes narrowed at Tae, recognition sparking in them—subtle but unmistakable.

Tae knew that look.

She turned to him.

"Are you… Park Tae-Joon? From Orion?"

Tae looked up. "Yes."

Her eyes widened.

"Oh, I thought so… I used to follow all your performances. 'Starlight' was my favorite—still on my playlist," she said, flushing slightly.

"I—I know this isn't the time, but… would it be okay to take a quick photo?"

Tae offered a faint smile. "Sure."

They stepped aside for a moment. She snapped a selfie, thanked him profusely, and bowed as she excused herself.

After she left, Mr. Baek turned to Tae with a stunned look.

"*Idol iyeyo?*"

(Are you an idol?)

"*Meotjeon iyeyo*," Tae said.

(A long time ago.)

"I'm a student now."

Hana cleared her throat gently, returning them to focus.

"Would it be all right if we spoke to the rest of your staff? Maybe walked the grounds ourselves?"

Mr. Baek nodded. "Yes, of course. You're welcome to speak with anyone and look around as needed. We'll give you full access. If there's anything we can do to help, please just ask."

He turned to Tae, his voice softening as he bowed again.

"Once again… I'm so very sorry for your loss. We were heartbroken to hear what happened."

Tae gave a small nod, not trusting himself to speak. He appreciated the man's words—he did—but each expression of sympathy felt like a pin pressed deeper into a wound that hadn't begun to close.

Talking about Sonia, speaking of her in the past tense, still felt surreal. As if he were narrating someone else's loss, not his own.

"Thank you," he replied politely. "I appreciate your help."

***

It was late in the evening.

Tae sat in the communal lounge of the guesthouse, nursing a mug of steaming green tea.

The ceilings were low, framed by dark timber beams, intersecting overhead. The walls were built from black volcanic stone, cool to the touch, their surface catching flickers of lamplight. Sliding doors covered in white *hanji*, traditional mulberry paper, framed the space, diffusing a soft glow from the adjacent hallway.

Several low tables sat scattered across the polished floor, each surrounded by floor cushions in faded earthy hues: ochre, rust, moss green. In one corner, a cast iron stove radiated steady warmth. Shelves lined with dog-eared travel books and mismatched ceramic teacups curved along the far wall.

There was something oddly timeless about the place—like it had slipped quietly out of the present and settled in a gentler era.

Outside, the sky had deepened to violet. The sea, visible beyond the swaying trees, was black and still.

Only one other guest shared the lounge with Tae—a woman in her sixties—seated a short distance away, a book open in her lap. She read slowly, her grey-blue deep set eyes, occasionally drifting from the page to study him with quiet interest.

She was Western, tall, lean, with short silver-blonde hair that curved slightly at the ends. Her skin was pale, lightly sunkissed in places, and delicately creased around the eyes and mouth.

When their gazes met, she offered a small smile.

Then Hana appeared, shrugging off her coat.

"Bap meogeosseoyo?" she asked.

(Have you eaten?)

"Not really."

"Baegopa jinjja," she said.

(I'm starving.)

156

"And you should eat too. I haven't seen you touch a thing all day."

She called the server over and ordered a spread for two: grilled tilefish, *haemul pajeon*, *abalone* porridge, and *kimchi* stew with tofu.

Tae watched her with quiet amusement.

She was already comfortable enough to order for both of them—and strangely, he didn't mind it. Somehow he found the gesture oddly comforting.

While they waited, Hana began straightening the cutlery with precise, deliberate care. Her movements were clean, measured, exact. It was her small, unconscious ritual, something Tae had come to recognize.

"Did you find anything?" he asked, watching her arrange the chopsticks, before moving on to the spoons.

Still straightening the spoons, Hana lowered her voice. "I spoke to the housekeeping staff. The bed in Sonia's room was untouched. Sheets and pillows weren't even wrinkled."

Tae stiffened, absorbing the information.

"I think she left for the cliff the same day she arrived," Hana concluded, now organizing the bowls.

"Then how did no one see her go?" Tae murmured, frowning.

Hana shrugged.

She looked up, meeting his eyes. "I don't know if they genuinely didn't notice—or if they're choosing not to speak. But everyone I spoke to seemed nervous."

She continued, "But then again... I get it. They've all already spoken to the police. Their boss confirmed seeing no one. So I doubt anyone's going to step forward now—not if it means risking their job."

The server returned, placing the food gently before them.

Warmth radiated from the clay bowls.

Hana's face lit up with unmistakable delight. It was a small, unguarded moment that caught Tae by surprise. There was something childlike about her happiness—unpretentious, instinctive.

He smiled, watching her eat.

"*Mwo?*" she asked, pausing mid-bite.

(What?)

"*Aniya,*" he said, still smiling.

(Nothing.)

"*Na eolgure mwo isseo?*"

(Something on my face?)

He shook his head

He noticed how she ate in a measured rhythm: three spoonfuls, pause; three more, pause; then another three. The pattern repeated like some private tempo.

"You're not eating," she said, suddenly noticing.

"Oh—yeah," he replied, and took a bite.

Just then, a soft voice interrupted them in careful Korean.

"*Gwaenchamyeon, yeogi anajido doelkka?*"

(May I join you?)

They both looked up. It was the silver-haired woman.

Her Korean was soft, accented, marked by years of effort.

"*Geureyo,*" Hana said, gesturing to the empty cushion beside them.

(Of course.)

The woman lowered herself onto it, gracefully.

"I couldn't help overhearing—you mentioned Sonia."

Both Hana and Tae looked at her, curiosity sparkling in their eyes.

Hana straightened. "*Aseu-eyo?*"

(Did you know her?)

"*Aju jal aneun geon anijiman.*"

(Not that well.)

"But we spoke briefly over breakfast. Being the only two foreigners, we naturally started talking."

She introduced herself: Eleanor Hayes, from Oregon.

Her husband, a Jeju-born doctor, had practiced in the U.S. They had returned together every year until his death. She now visited the island alone to stay few months each year, out of ritual.

"She was beautiful," Eleanor said, looking now at the news article about Sonia on Hana's phone. "I was shocked to hear what happened to her. She was so young…"

Eleanor's voice trailed off.

Tae said nothing.

"She mentioned someone she loved," Eleanor continued gently.

"*Neo-ya?*" she said, directly gazing at Tae.

(Was it you?)

Tae nodded.

"I guessed as much. The way she described you, I could tell it was *you* when I saw you here today. She told me you were extremely handsome. I thought she must be exaggerating. But I see now… she wasn't."

Tae gave a small, awkward smile.

"You were going to be married?" Eleanor asked.

"Yes, we were engaged," Tae replied.

Eleanor nodded, unsurprised.

"She showed me her ring—a rose pink diamond. Said she was here to surprise you for your birthday. She seemed so happy."

Tae pulled out his phone and showed her a photo of the ring. Eleanor peered at it, and then nodded.

"*Eung, geugeoya.*"

(Yes. That's the one.)

Hana leaned in. "Did you see anyone with her that day? We've been asking around, but no one seems to know anything."

Eleanor paused, thinking.

Then after a few seconds, she said:

"Yes... *geureon geot gat-ayo.*"

(I believe I did.)

Tae and Hana straightened.

Eleanor hesitated. "You see, I didn't get a clear look. I was sitting in the lounge. But I remember someone meeting her outside. A woman."

"*Geunyeoga eottaesseo?*" Hana asked, voice tight with urgency.

(Can you describe her?)

"I believe she was petite, slim... about your height," she said, nodding toward Hana

"She was facing away from me. So, I couldn't see her face. But she wore some kind of red hoodie and leggings. I just remember the two of them standing outside... then leaving together in a car."

"Can you remember the make of the car?"

Eleanor frowned.

"Black. Large... like one of those Land Rover types. Maybe a Kia Mohave? Something bulky."

Tae's pulse kicked.

"Did Sonia seem uneasy? Nervous? Like she didn't want to go."

Eleanor shook her head.

160

"No. Not at all. In fact, she was smiling. She looked... excited."

Hana pressed on.

"Is there anything else you remember? Anything unusual? Even the smallest thing can help."

Eleanor hesitated.

"No, I don't think so... nothing clear. Just that the woman was wearing all black, and that they left in a SUV."

Then suddenly, she looked up, eyes bright—as if struck by a fragment of memory.

"Wait... there was something. On her arm."

She touched her own forearm.

"Right here. Just beneath the sleeve."

"I only saw it for a second when she briefly lifted her arm. But it looked like a tattoo of some kind."

"What kind of tattoo?" Hana asked quickly.

"I couldn't see the details clearly, but it was red. Bright red. That's what stood out to me. Most tattoos are black, but this one—the red was so vivid. I remember thinking *that's* a striking color."

"Do you remember the shape?"

Eleanor closed her eyes briefly.

"Hmm... some kind of flower, I think. I only saw it from a distance, but... yes, it looked like a flower."

Tae and Hana exchanged a glance.

A red flower.

Not a name.

Not a face.

But something.

A thread in the dark.

And finally—something to follow.

Chapter 14

[Suggested Soundtrack: *"From the Beginning Until Now" by Ryu. Press play when the song appears in the chapter.*]

THE OLD TV CRACKLED softly as it filled the apartment with a warm, flickering glow.

In the spotless fictional living room of *Rainbow Family*, the Lee family was already bustling with energy.

"Jiho-ya!" the mother called brightly, poking her head out from behind the sliding kitchen door, her voice light and chipper.

"Guess what today is?"

Jiho, home from school and still in his school uniform, looked up from his comic book, eyes gleaming.

"Eomma! Seolma Appa saengsineun anijyo?"

(Eomma! Don't tell me it's Appa's birthday?)

She shook her head with a laugh, her floral apron tied neatly around her waist as she stepped into view, holding a bundle of fresh scallions.

"Not yet. But it's still special. Today, we're going to surprise him when he comes home!"

Jiho's eyes lit up.

"Appa ga jeil joahaneun geu bap?"

(With his favorite dish?)

She nodded with exaggerated importance.

"*Geurae.*"

(That's right.)

She beamed. "Your father's had a hard week. I thought we'd make his favorite—*galbijjim*, just the way Halmeoni used to make it. What do you say?"

Jiho sprang up from the couch, already rolling up his sleeves, then paused mid-motion, tilting his head and squinting with mock seriousness.

"Wait… Eomma, didn't Appa get a stomach ache the last time you made that?"

She blinked. "Eh?"

Jiho adopted a solemn tone, as if relaying a grave national emergency.

"You remember! He missed poker night with Mr. Choi and spent the evening holding his tummy and making weird noises in the bathroom!"

Eomma's eyes widened in mock horror as the memory hit her.

"*Aigoo!* That's right! After that, he didn't touch *cheongjang gochu* for a week!"

She clapped her hand over her mouth.

"Every time I mentioned it, he ran straight to the bathroom faster than the bus *ajusshi!*"

The audience burst into laughter.

Eomma and Nari laughed too.

They were curled up together on the floor in front of the TV, watching with wide, glowing eyes.

Eomma's hands worked gently through Nari's long black hair, weaving it into soft pigtails. The brush moving in a rhythm that never broke—slow, tender, and full of love.

Jiho grinned at his mother on-screen.

"Don't worry, Eomma," he declared. "This time it'll be perfect—because I will help you. I'll be your sous chef!"

"Oh ho—my little sous chef!" his mother cooed, patting his cheek.

"Well then, let's make Appa proud—and keep him out of the bathroom!"

Just then Appa popped in on screen, stepping into the house with flowers in one hand and a paper bag in the other.

"My ear is itchy. Were you two talking about me?" he said with a grin.

The audience burst into laughter.

He leaned in and kissed his wife's cheek, gently placing the bouquet in her hands.

The mother on-screen beamed, clearly smitten.

"Oh! My favorite flowers!" she gasped.

"But... what's the occasion?"

"Do I need an occasion to celebrate my beautiful wife?" the father charmingly said with a wink.

On the other side of the screen, Eomma's eyes lit up.

The audience cooed, as soft romantic music played beneath the laughter.

The show ended with a cheerful reminder to tune in next week, as Eomma reached forward and turned off the TV.

A shy smile tugged at the corners of her lips.

She looked down at Nari and said, "You know... these days your Abeoji... he's been just like that Appa on screen. Just yesterday—he got me flowers."

She gestured toward the dresser where a bouquet of pale pink roses sat in a glass jar.

"*Igeo-do sajwasseo*," she said, opening a drawer and lifting out a small box.

(He also got me this.)

Inside was a delicate mother-of-pearl watch.

Nari's eyes widened.

"It's something I've always dreamed of having," she says, her voice tinged with longing. "I thought he'd forgotten after all these years… but I guess he hasn't."

She giggled like a schoolgirl, brushing her fingers along her cheek.

"It's like we're back in our school days. Like I'm seeing him for the first time again."

A beautiful smile lit up Eomma's face, and Nari couldn't help but smile too. It had been a long time since she'd seen her mother this happy.

She had also noticed that Abeoji had changed since the day those bad men left. He had been kinder, sweeter, gentler—not only with Eomma but also with her. A sharp change from before when he would get angry whenever Eomma so much as mentioned her name or said anything about her.

"Go put on that blue dress I got you," Eomma said, her voice light. "It's almost seven—he'll be back any minute, and he wants us to be ready when he arrives. We're going out today. I should get ready too."

Nari opened the cupboard and carefully pulled out the dress—sky blue, with soft white lace tracing the hem like delicate clouds.

Eomma too began to dress. She chose her best—a hanbok-inspired chiffon midi dress in soft pastel pink. The skirt flowed gently below the knee, light as air, while the white wrap-style bodice echoed the lines of a jeogori, its cuffs delicately embroidered with pale thread. The pink ribbon at her waist was tied off to one side.

Her hair fell loose over her shoulders. And as a final touch, she added a pair of delicate pearl earrings.

"He gave me these too," she murmured, admiring her reflection in the mirror as she showed them to Nari.

She looked luminous.

There was a knock on the door.

"*Geu sarami bunmyeonghae*," Eomma said, her voice tinged with excitement.

(It must be him.)

They walked to the door together.

Abeoji stood in the hallway, waiting.

But they could hardly recognize him.

Eomma nearly stepped back at the sight of Abeoji, and even Nari stood frozen, stunned.

He was clean-shaven, dressed in a crisp suit, a bouquet of flowers in one hand and bags of takeout in the other. He looked... different... like the Appa from *Rainbow Family*.

Eomma's hand flew to her mouth in shock.

"*Jinjja neo majji?*" she said, staring at him.

(Is that really you?)

"*Museun il isseosseo?*"

(What happened?)

Abeoji smiled gently, a hint of mischief in his eyes.

"Can't a man look handsome for his wife?" he said softly, with a smile.

He even sounded like Appa from *Rainbow Family*.

"Let's have dinner first," he said gently. "We'll go out after."

He stepped inside, the scent of the evening clinging to his suit, and laid the bags gently on the low dining table. One by one, he unpacked the boxes—*kimchi jjigae* still steaming in its container, glossy strands of *japchae* slick with sesame oil, golden fried shrimp nestled beside a small dish of tangy dipping sauce.

For Nari, there was a generous portion of *tteokbokki*, rice cakes glistening in a rich, red *gochujang* glaze. And for dessert, two *hotteok*—crispy at the edges, warm and soft in the center—oozing with brown sugar and honey.

Eomma stared at the spread, her hand hovering just above her heart. The dishes weren't just delicious: they were thoughtful.

Kimchi jjigae and *japchae* had always been her favorites, ever since their early days of dating. The shrimp and *tteokbokki* were exactly what Nari adored. The kind of food Eomma wished she could treat Nari to on birthdays or special occasions, but wasn't always able to.

Suddenly a look of concern appeared on her face.

"Listen… can we afford all this? Where is all this money coming from?" she asked quietly, her voice caught between awe and worry.

Abeoji looked at her, then at Nari, who was already inching closer to the table, eyes wide.

"Don't worry about it," he said softly, settling onto the floor beside her. "Remember that interview? They called back. It's official—I got the job! They even gave me an advance today."

Eomma's lips parted, but no words came.

Her eyes brimmed with tears—this time, not from fear or pain, but relief and joy. She tried to hold them back, but they spilled over anyway, streaking down her cheeks in silence.

Abeoji reached out, his fingers gently brushing her face as he wiped the tears away, one by one.

"*Ulji ma*," he murmured. "Everything's going to be better now. I promise."

(Don't cry.)

Eomma's voice trembled. "But… what about those men?"

"Don't worry, I spoke to them," he said, his tone firm but calm. "I gave them a portion of the advance. They won't be coming to the house again. They won't scare us anymore."

"Now," he said, looking between Eomma and Nari, his eyes bright, "let's celebrate the good news tonight, shall we?"

He reached into one of the bags and pulled out a small green bottle of soju, then poured it carefully into two shallow glasses—one for himself, one for Eomma. For Nari, he held up a chilled bottle of banana milk with a smile, the way one might raise a toast.

"*Geonbae, yeobo*," he said softly.

(Cheers, honey.)

They clinked glasses. Then, as he reached for his chopsticks, he paused and tapped his forehead.

"Oh wait—I forgot the side dishes," he said.

"*Geumbang olge.*"

(Be right back.)

He stood up and disappeared into the kitchen

Nari took a few bites of the *tteokbokki* and sipped at the banana milk. But after a moment, she set the bottle down and gently pushed both the drink and plate slightly away, her appetite waning.

Eomma noticed.

"Not hungry?" she asked softly.

Nari gave a small shake of her head, her gaze falling to the table.

Eomma glanced toward the kitchen, making sure Abeoji

was still out of earshot. Then, leaning in with a faint, knowing smile, she whispered, "But he got it for us… it wouldn't be nice to waste it."

She reached over and quietly took the remaining *tteokbokki* from Nari's plate, then lifted the bottle of banana milk and drank Nari's share herself.

Just then, Abeoji returned from the kitchen, carrying a small metal tray lined with *banchan*: neatly stacked sheets of seasoned kimchi, glossy strands of spinach dressed in sesame oil; and pale pickled radish.

He set them down with care.

After the meal, he rose and stretched, then turned to Eomma with a smile.

"Let's go for a drive," he said. "You remember how much you used to love those late-night rides when we first got the car? I haven't done that in a while."

He hesitated for a breath, then added quietly, "I'm sorry. I haven't always been a good husband to you. But I want to make up for it. I'll do better from now on. I promise."

Eomma blinked, her lashes glistening.

She looked up at him, lips trembling, and nodded.

"*Gwaenchanha*," she whispered.

(It's okay.)

They stepped outside together.

The air was cool, the sky dark and cloudless.

He unlocked the car—an old, compact Kia Morning, the paint slightly dulled, the edges worn with age. It was nothing fancy, but it ran smooth and steady.

Eomma took the passenger seat. Nari climbed into the back, her small hands gripping the door handle, holding on to it like an anchor, eyes wide with curiosity.

The windows were rolled down, and a gentle breeze drifted in, carrying the scent of the night—earthy, crisp, laced with the faint tang of the city.

As they slipped into the glowing heart of the city, he reached for the stereo and pressed play.

A soft melody filled the car—familiar, aching, beautiful.

"From the Beginning Until Now," by Ryu.

One of Eomma's favorites.

She turned to him slowly, her eyes wide and glistening.

"Gieokhaetgun," she whispered.

(You remembered.)

He gave a quiet nod, a smile tugging at the corners of his lips.

They drove on in silence for a while, save the music drifting through the car and the steady hum of the engine filling the quiet.

Lights blurred outside: neon signs, streetlamps, the occasional flicker of headlights streaking past.

Then, without a word, he reached over, took her hand gently in his, and kissed it.

She blinked, startled by the gesture, by the unfamiliar tenderness of it, as if her body no longer knew how to receive something so loving.

It was such a simple gesture, and yet it stirred something long asleep inside her.

He hadn't touched her like that in years.

"Saranghae," he whispered.

(I love you.)

And in that single moment, something in her chest gave way—a quiet, aching crack.

That one word carried everything.

It seemed to reach across all the pain they had borne, all the hurt they'd lived through... all the years they had lost and couldn't get back.

Tears gathered before she realized.

They slipped down Eomma's cheek.

She didn't brush them away.

Her hand rose slowly as she cupped his face with a tenderness that held years of ache and quiet hope inside it. Her thumb brushed gently along the curve of his jaw, as if tracing something once familiar—something that had never truly left her.

From the corner of his eye, a single tear broke free and wandered down his face.

For a moment, neither of them moved.

They stayed like that for the rest of the drive, hands entwined, as if holding on to something precious.

The music swirled around them—tender, luminous, steeped in memory—folding over them like a soft shawl, weaving the past and present together.

From the backseat, Nari watched quietly.

Abeoji's gaze kept returning to Eomma: steady, full of wonder.

It was the same look from the old school photo Eomma once showed her—the one where he stood beside her in his uniform, staring at her like she was the only thing in the world that mattered.

Her mother's eyes shimmered with joy. Her father looked younger somehow, almost boyish in the way he gazed at Eomma.

Nari's heart swelled.

She smiled without meaning to.

The night air drifted in through the open windows—cool, sweet, scented faintly with salt and mist.

The city was behind them now, its hum fading as its lights dimmed to a distant glow.

Nari's eyelids fluttered.

The melody wrapped around her like a lullaby.

As she drifted into sleep, the smile stayed.

Just like *Rainbow Family*, she thought.

They were perfect now.

Just like the show.

Finally… they were whole.

***

She woke to cold.

Not the kind that gently brushes against the skin—

but something deeper.

A creeping chill that seeped through the fabric of her clothes, into her flesh, between her ribs—settling in her bones and staying there.

Something was wrong.

The air was too still.

The silence, too thick.

The world… tilted.

Then came the sound—

A low groan, deep and metallic,

Like something old and heavy giving way.

Sea water.

Black

Rising.
Seeping in through the windows—
Slow, soundless, certain.
The car was sinking.
Her heart slammed against her chest.
Thud-thud-thud.
The panic began with that sound.
Beneath it, she could hear the groan of metal under pressure.
The car frame tightening.
The seat belt dug into her chest like a wire.
The cold climbed, inch by inch.
Creeping up her legs like frost.
Wrapping around her knees.
And higher and higher… slowly consuming her.
She looked up front.
Eomma sat slumped on the passenger seat, still.
Not asleep.
Not awake.
Her hair floated slightly, already touched by the rising tide.
In the driver's seat, Abeoji rested against the window.
Eyes closed.
His hands had slipped from the wheel, palms open.
No one moved.
No one breathed.
The water pressed against her waist now—
Like hands.
She reached for the door handle.
Pulled.
Nothing.
Again—harder.
Still nothing.

The lock wouldn't budge.
Her small fists struck the door.
Once.
Twice.
Again.
The water surged higher.
Higher.
Clawing up her chest, her neck.
It burned now—where it touched her skin.
Outside, the sea was a black veil.
No lights. No moon. No stars.
Only black.
Nari looked at her mother.
At her father.
At their stillness.
And then—
She screamed.
One sound.
Sharp. Piercing.
Raw and ripping—torn from somewhere beneath language.
The scream of a child who wanted to live.
But no one heard her.
She opened her mouth.
And the sea rushed in.
Cold. Unrelenting.
It filled her mouth, her nose, her throat.
Her lungs screamed for air—began to spasm.
The car sank lower.
And lower still.
Dragged downward
By hands she could not see.

The silence thickened.
Until it was just her.
And the sea.

Chapter 15

7:00 A.M

"ONE, TWO, THREE, FOUR. Two, two, three, four..."

The counts echoed through the mirrored dance studio buried in the basement of Onyx Entertainment's building.

The six girls of the K-pop group Nyx sashayed forward in a triangle formation as their hit song "Midnight," a sultry synth-pop track, blared through the loudspeakers.

Serina led the group, as the other girls fanned behind her like the wings of a blade. Six bodies in sync—sharp, fluid, controlled—their hands slicing the air in choreographed precision.

The air in the studio was dense with the scent of linoleum and sweat, undercut only by a faint trace of vanilla-scented disinfectant sprayed just enough to keep up appearances.

Black speakers lined the walls. On one side, shelves held microphones, neatly stacked bags, and water bottles.

Mirrors wrapped around the room, reflecting the idols'

176

slender frames—long lines etched into motion—multiplied endlessly in the glass.

A middle-aged man stood at the front, his eyes tracking the girls' every move with razor focus: silent, arms folded, expression unreadable.

He was their choreographer, dressed in Adidas track pants and a Yankees cap pulled low over his brow. A whistle hung from his neck as a badge of authority.

Serina's muscles burned with a familiar ache. Her leggings clung to her frame, sweat already glistening at her collarbone beneath a cropped black hoodie.

Around her, the other girls wore variations of rehearsal gear—hoodies with leggings, sweatshirts and shorts, crop tops paired with ripped jeans—each gripping a mic as they lip synced to the beat.

They slipped into their invisible stage personas as they whipped their hair, swayed their hips, and shimmied with practiced ease. All of it performed atop pointed high heels that struck the polished wood floor like weapons.

Fatigue clung to their faces and bodies—the toll of sixteen-hour days packed with choreography run-throughs, vocal drills, interviews, and late-night fan-cams—sustained by barely four hours of sleep.

But they masked it well.

Small, practiced smiles played on each of their lips, identical rehearsed expressions, that never reached their eyes.

As the song ended, the six of them came together in a final pose—shoulders rising, chests lifted. Six figures frozen in motion. Three of them dropped low to one knee in front, while the other three posed above them, curves angled, limbs taut.

A perfect frame of seduction.

The choreographer's whistle split the air.

"Gamjeong! Gamjeongi piryohae!"

(Emotions! I need emotions!)

He took a step forward, scowling.

"Your faces look dead. How can you dance without feeling?"

"Geurae, majji?" he asked, looking around the room—expecting an answer.

(Am I right?)

"Ne," they replied in unison—their tone flat.

(Yes.)

He jabbed a finger at the wall of mirrors.

"Then look *carefully*! Pay attention to your shoulders, your hands, your legs. You need to *feel* every single movement!"

"Dasi!"

(Again!)

The track rewound.

The commanding voice returned.

"One, two, three, four. Two, two, three, four..."

Sharp heels stabbed the floor.

Serina's arms burned, her body trembled, her breath strained—but she kept going.

The whistle shrieked again.

The room froze.

He pointed at Yena.

"Neo—naege boyeojwo."

(You—show me.)

Yena stepped forward, clad in black biker shorts under an oversized white tee. Her hair was slicked into a bun. At the cue, she hit the pivot-step: hip rolling in a smooth arc, arms lifting skyward in one fluid motion.

178

"Aniya. Geureon shik-i aniya."

(No. Not like that.)

*"Heel-ro bal cha! Ireohge—*bam!*"* He demonstrated, stamping the ground with sharp emphasis.

(Step with your heel! Like this—bam!)

She repeated it.

Again.

And again.

And again.

Finally, he gave the barest nod.

"You'd better have it perfect by the end of the day!" he barked.

The music resumed.

"One, two, three, four. Two, two, three, four..."

The girls moved in high heels, their faces blank with focus—drained but mechanical—like clockwork dolls wound up once more.

***

1:00 P.M.

Serina stood inside the booth.

The recording studio was bathed in dim orange light. In front of her, a sleek, oversized black condenser microphone loomed. A fine metal mesh grille capped the top like a net, designed to catch every breath, every imperfection.

Padded studio headphones clamped over her ears enclosing her in a private world—the opening bars of their new track, "Lover Boy," reverberated through the silence.

"You are my lover. Like no other. Let's be together, baby..."

179

Serina crooned the first line of the song, her voice breathy, tinged with the faintest lilt of an accent.

Behind the glass, the producer watched in silence.

Thick-rimmed glasses reflected the blue glow of the monitor in front of him.

He took a drag of his cigarette and exhaled slowly, smoke curling toward the ceiling like a lazy ghost.

"Baby' hanbeon deo hae," his voice instructed, crackling through the intercom.

(Do "baby" one more time.)

"Malhae... bay−bee. Neoreul kkeullyeo."

(Say... bay-bee. Stretch it out.)

Serina nodded.

She inhaled softly and leaned into the mic.

"You are my lover. Like no other. Let's be together, bay-bee..."

"Do it again. You're lacking power."

She gave a small nod, eyes flicking briefly toward the control room window where the producer sat like a shadow behind the glass, and sang again.

The producer tapped his pen against the console, lips pursed.

"You sound flat. Pull yourself together. Put some energy into it."

"Choego-ro hago isseoyo."

(I'm giving it my best.)

"Geureom deo johgeona."

(Then make it better.)

"Dasi," he prompted.

(Again.)

"Start from the low note."

She braced herself, letting the silence linger in her chest for a breath longer than usual.

Then, she sang once more—more breath, more grit, more ache.

Finally, through the static of the intercom, his voice came.

"Choya... okay."

(Good... okay.)

***

8:00 P.M.

"Look sexy. Look cute. But *not* stupid."

Director Moon's words landed like bullets, slicing through the silence like a gavel.

The only other sound was the low hum of the air conditioner.

The six girls of Nyx sat on one side of a sterile metal conference table in the fifth floor of the building. Their bodies slouched with exhaustion, but their eyes were bright and alert, with fear, they didn't dare show.

Overhead, bright lights buzzed down. Director Moon sat alone on the other side of the table.

It felt less like a meeting—and more like an interrogation.

Moon wore a blindingly white pantsuit, pressed to perfection, which clung to her rigid frame. Her jet-black bob framed her face. Her lips, painted maroon, were unsmiling.

She did not sit. She towered.

"Image is *everything*," she said—her mantra, repeated like scripture.

Director Moon's eyes swept the table.

"To be an idol, you must master your image. It is your most critical asset. Never forget that."

Moon crossed her arms.

181

"Do you want to look stupid in interviews?" she snapped.

The girls shook their heads in silence.

One of them nervously twirled a half-finished water bottle. Another jotted something in her notebook, her pen scratching against the page.

Serina looked around at the others—she kept her back straight, her expression blank.

Moon turned to Minseo.

"Member composition?"

Minseo recited the answer like a prayer.

"Our member composition aims to emphasize our strength in beauty and our diversity. We all come from different backgrounds. Some of us aspire to be models. Some hope to act. Some of us want to be singers. We work together to balance our unique strengths. Together we are one—we are Nyx."

Moon gave a brief nod, then turned her gaze to Ara.

"What's the meaning behind your group's name?"

Ara hesitated.

"Um… Nyx is… a Greek goddess. Of the night. Because our group is… kind of dark and sexy. That was the concept… I think…"

Her voice trailed off.

The silence that followed was thick enough to suffocate.

Director Moon's face hardened.

"Didn't I give you all a deadline to have this memorized?"

"*Mianhaeyo, seonsaengnim,*" Ara whispered.

(I'm sorry, teacher.)

Moon's eyes narrowed on Serina.

"And *you*. You're the leader," she said, her tone turning cold and hard.

"*Jal chaeng-gyeo-ya dwae.*"

(Are you taking care of them?)

"You are supposed to make sure they are ready. Aren't you watching over your members?"

Serina said nothing. Her eyes lowered. Her hands rested on her knees, clenched tight.

"*Leedeo-neun geunyang jireum-i aniya.*"

(Leader is not just a title.)

Tears gathered quietly at the corners of Serina's eyes. She willed them not to fall.

She should be used to this by now. But five years in, the words still stung.

It was *always* like this. When something slipped, when someone forgot—

The leader took the fall.

The worst part was: the other girls believed it too.

Maybe not out of malice.

Maybe just out of convenience.

No one ever asked who was really at fault.

No one cared.

It was always Serina.

***

9:36 P.M.

The hallway smelled of bleach and metal. Serina was on her way out of Onyx Entertainment—when her phone vibrated in her hand.

Two texts from Jaeho:

"*Apollo-ro wa.*"

(Come to Apollo's.)

"Neoreul wihan surprise-ga isseo."

(I have a surprise for you.)

Her face broke into a warm smile—her first genuine smile of the day.

She typed back quickly:

"Gago isseo."

(Coming.)

Then she slid her phone into her pocket, stepped outside, and hailed a cab.

***

Cheongdam-dong, Seoul

10.30 P.M.

Apollo shimmered like sin.

It wasn't just a restaurant—it was a stage.

And Serina had just walked into the spotlight.

Inside, the air was thick with perfume and cigar smoke. Coils of purple-gold lights flashed across the ceiling like a living flame, casting soft reflections on the glossy black marble floor.

Bass pulsed through the floor in deep, sensual waves.

Waitstaff drifted by, with trays of champagne fizzing in tall gold-tipped glasses.

A hostess ushered Serina to a private room, draped in velvet, lined with gilded mirrors, and low plush couches that looked too expensive to sit on.

And there, at the center of it all, her eyes fell on—

184

Tae.

Her crush. Her ultimate idol. Her bias.

He looked unreal.

An electric blue shirt clung to his broad shoulders; his midnight black trousers tailored to perfection. His hair was tousled just enough to look effortless. Under the warm lights, his skin seemed to glow.

He looked up at her—and Serina froze.

Her knees felt weak, but she kept her face composed.

He was everything she had imagined, and somehow even more than that.

She'd only seen him in photos, on screens, and from faraway stages.

She knew he was handsome—that was common knowledge.

But in person, he was… breathtaking.

The rumors that had swirled about his looks through practice rooms and dorm corridors during her trainee days weren't exaggerated.

If anything, they had fallen short.

Beside him, Jaeho greeted her with a crooked grin. He wore a sleek white blazer over a black turtleneck, his hair styled to casual perfection.

His eyes glinted with amusement, clearly enjoying her barely concealed awe.

"Tae, this is Serina," he said, introducing her. "She's the leader and main vocalist of Nyx. Their song 'Midnight' is killing it right now."

"And," he added with a smirk, "she also happens to be a huge fan of yours."

Serina's face flushed red.

Tae gave her a soft smile and a small nod.

185

Serina bowed, painfully aware of how underdressed she was in her most casual post-practice outfit—an old beige off-shoulder top tucked into a pair of high-waist jeans, tattered in places from regular wear. Her ponytail was barely holding together.

"Oppa, if I'd known… I would've dressed better."

"*Gwaenchanha boyeo*," Jaeho said, smiling.

(You look fine.)

"*Baegopa? Meogeul geo isseo?*" he asked, motioning at the food on the table.

(Hungry? Want anything to eat?)

Serina surveyed the spread, her eyes shining with a mix of hunger and longing: grilled *galbi*, *japchae*, *bulgogi*, fresh strawberries, and slices of cheesecake.

Her mouth filled with saliva. Her stomach clenched.

She hadn't eaten all day—save a banana for breakfast, a single boiled egg for lunch, and a green protein shake awaiting her at dinner.

It had been that way for the last two months.

She shook her head, looking away from the food.

"Weigh-in tomorrow," she murmured, voice barely audible. "I didn't make the cutoff last time."

Her face burned with shame.

At five foot seven and 110 pounds—50 kilos—Serina wasn't fat. Not by any normal standard.

But the agency's rule was strict: 49 kilograms or under.

No exceptions. It didn't matter how tall you were.

Every Friday morning, the girls were weighed in the practice room—one by one—in front of everyone.

No privacy.

No mercy.

The numbers on the scale were read aloud like a verdict.

Failing the weekly weigh-in didn't just mean public humiliation and censure in front of everyone—it meant punishment—anything from weeks of extra cardio, stricter calorie restrictions, additional rounds of dance practice. Or worse: being benched from shoots altogether.

Last week, Serina had stood there in nothing but her underwear—in front of their manager, group members, and the Onyx Entertainment staff—and failed the cutoff by a single kilogram.

The members who had gone before her had all made the cutoff—each one stepping off the scale in squeals of joy, arms flung around each other in giddy relief.

But when Serina's number was announced, the room went quiet.

That silence had been louder than any reprimand.

She'd felt the eyes of the other girls on her: cautious, pitying, but mostly just grateful it wasn't them. That had been the worst humiliation for her, especially in front of her group.

She was the leader. She *had* to be perfect.

Jaeho gave her a look of sympathy. "We had to do that too. Back during our trainee days."

Tae leaned forward slightly.

"Don't take that too seriously," he said gently. "Just focus on your talent and work hard. That's all that matters."

"This other stuff?" he added. "It won't last. So, take care of your health."

Serina looked down, blinking fast.

Hearing those kind words of encouragement—from someone she had admired for years—made something tighten in her chest. It almost made her want to cry.

Just then, Rian entered the room, the doors closing behind him.

"Where were you?" Jaeho asked, half teasing.

"I invited Tae to your restaurant after his return from Jeju, so we could all catch up—and you show up *now*?"

Rian grinned, unapologetic.

"Sorry... had to charm a few VIPs. You know how it is."

"Of course," Jaeho said, laughing. "You're a big-shot businessman now."

He turned to Tae. "Have you been to his newest club?"

"Red Moon. It's the hottest spot in Gangnam right now. Two-hour waits just to get in—and don't even get me started on the cover charge."

Tae shook his head.

"Not for everyone," Rian chimed in, flashing a smirk. "If you're pretty like Serina—there's no cover," he said with a laugh.

Serina gave a small, demure smile, lowering her gaze for a beat before looking up again.

"But seriously, you should drop in sometime," Rian said, nudging Tae.

"If the word gets out you're there—half the city would line up just to catch a glimpse of you. It's a win-win."

"Pretty sure that's only a win for one person," Jaeho laughed, pointing at Rian.

"I'm not really into clubs," Tae replied. "I don't even drink now. Been off it for a while."

"*Mwo?*" Rian said, mock-offended.

(What?)

"But I ordered the best bottle in the house in your honor."

From the ice bucket beside him, Rian lifted the dark green

188

bottle of 2009 DomPérignon Brut Methuselah and poured Tae a glass.

Tae reluctantly took a polite sip, before setting the glass down with care.

Then, almost hesitantly, he asked, "How come Duri didn't come?"

Jaeho gave a small shrug.

"I did invite him. Even told him you were back in Seoul. But he said he was busy."

"Still with the label?"

Jaeho shook his head. "No. He stepped away from the idol world a year after you left. These days, he's focused on his art. We barely see him. I'm hoping he'll at least show up for my engagement reception."

Rian leaned back, resting his arm along the back of his chair.

"Last time I saw him was at his exhibition last year. My wife and I bought one of his pieces. He's become... reclusive. Keeps to himself, pretty much."

"I tried inviting him to a few things," Rian continued. "Openings, Christmas, birthdays. He never showed. After a while... I stopped trying."

Tae nodded slowly.

The answer wasn't surprising—and yet it felt heavy. It was another reminder of how far they'd all drifted apart.

Just then, Serina's phone buzzed.

Ten missed calls.

Her smile faded.

"*Jamshiman-yo,*" she said softly, rising from the velvet couch and heading to the restroom.

(Excuse me.)

***

Inside the restroom, she ducked into a stall, locked the door, and stared at the screen.

Her phone lit up as it rang again.

She hesitated, then answered.

"Where the hell are you? Why weren't you picking up my calls?" an angry male voice thundered.

Serina flinched.

It was Yunji—her secret boyfriend.

They had been seeing each other quietly for nearly a year.

No one at the agency knew. Not the manager. Not the staff. Not even her group members.

Her contract strictly forbade dating, and a scandal would end her career as an idol.

"*Naneun Apollo-ya,*" she said, keeping her voice steady.

(I'm at Apollo.)

"Just having dinner."

"*Nugu?*" His voice was sharp, already suspicious.

(With who?)

"*Geunyang chingudeul.*"

(Just some friends.)

"*Geojitmal.*" he snapped.

(Lies.)

"I called all your friends. No one knows where you are."

Serina's throat tightened.

She hesitated, then admitted quietly:

"Jaeho-oppa invited me."

Silence.

Then his voice returned—low, cold.

"*Nae-ga. Jigeum.*"

190

(Leave. Now.)

A pause.

"Or I'll do something you'll regret."

"*Jebal, jagiya—*" Serina began.

(Please, baby.)

Click.

The line went dead.

She stared at the screen, her reflection flickering across the dark glass. Her heart pounded in her ears.

***

Back at the table, she tried to keep her voice steady, though her hands trembled slightly.

"*Biane,*" she said.

(Sorry.)

"Something urgent came up."

"*Naneun gaya dwae.*"

(I have to go.)

Jaeho stood up, his expression tight.

"Was it him? Did he call again?"

She nodded faintly. "I'm sorry."

"*Naega dowajulge—*"

(Let me help—)

"*Ani,*" she said quickly, her voice catching, just slightly.

(No.)

"*Gomawo. Jinjja. Hajiman naneun gaya dwae.*"

(Thank you. Really. But I have to go.)

She bowed politely to Tae and the others, then rushed out.

As the door closed behind her, Jaeho glanced around the table.

"She's with Yunji," he said quietly. "From Riot12."

His tone darkened.

"He's insanely possessive. She called me once, crying— begged me to cover for her."

Rian frowned.

"Yunji? I've seen him at Red Moon a few times. I didn't know they were dating. He seemed into some of the other girls at the club—I figured he was single."

Tae turned to Jaeho.

"How do you know her?"

"She was close to Mino," Jaeho said.

"They're both vocalists, and so she really looked up to him. During her trainee days, she leaned on him a lot. Saw him like a big brother."

Tae blinked. *"Geunyeoga geureotda-go?"*

(She did?)

Jaeho nodded slowly. "Actually… she was one of the last people to see him. They met up the night before he—"

He stopped himself.

A heavy silence descended over the table. No one said another word.

Tae didn't speak either, but he made a mental note to follow up with Hana.

Maybe Serina knew something.

***

Apgujeong-dong, Seoul

12:00 A.M.

The apartment greeted her with silence.

Outside, the muffled hum of Seoul's nightlife filtered faintly through the windows: distant engines, an occasional burst of laughter, the low throb of music from passing cars.

The air held a mix of lingering scents: lavender face cream, instant ramen, shampoo, and the faint musk of laundry detergent.

The studio was no bigger than a practice room. A thin mattress lay crumpled on the floor. Sticky notes papered the walls. Affirmations scrawled in Sharpie. Calorie goals, tallied with clinical precision. A timetable, broken down to the hour.

Serina shared the space with two other group members. Both of them were out today, visiting family.

She slipped into the bathroom.

The light buzzed softly overhead, flickering once before settling into a pale, uneven glow over the small, tiled space.

Serina raised her phone, angled it carefully, and snapped a quick selfie—her face half-shadowed, expression calm, composed.

She sent it to Yunji with a simple caption.

"Jib-e dowaesseo."

(Just got home.)

A few minutes passed.

Then a soft ping.

He'd hearted the photo.

She let out a quiet breath she hadn't realized she was holding, then tied her hair into a loose knot and turned on the faucet.

Cold water splashed against her skin. She scrubbed her face—harder than necessary, as if trying to wash off the weight of the day

She looked up.

The mirror had a crack in the corner. A small note clung to its surface in pink ink:

"Haengbokhae."

(Be happy.)

A small heart was drawn beside it—now faint and fading.

Her desk was located in the corner of the room, neatly organized, with her make up, brushes, a MacBook, and a red notebook.

She opened the laptop. The screen flickered to life.

Her desktop wallpaper appeared—she stared at it.

A photo of her, Mino and Harin.

Laughing. Happy. Alive.

Two of them were gone now.

Only she remained.

Her hand reached toward the screen, fingers hovering over Mino's face.

"Biane, Oppa," she whispered.

(I'm sorry, Oppa.)

"Jebal yongseohae."

(Please forgive me.)

She hesitated. Then fingers trembling, she typed something into the search bar.

The browser loaded.

As Serina leaned in, her fabric shifted. . . just for a second.

A flash of red.

A rose. Blood-red.

Barely visible beneath the edge of her sleeve—

Inked delicately on the inside of her forearm.

Vivid. Startling. Stark against her pale skin.

She traced it with her fingertips, her gaze locked on the screen.

A photo of Sonia.

Epilogue

FOR THREE DAYS, SHE had haunted the shore—a feral slip of a girl—all hollow limbs and wind-chapped skin, barely more than bone and breath.

Now she wandered the coastline, a ruin shaped like a child, hair matted with brine, cheeks sunken, feet blistered raw from sea-worn stones, knees skinned from coral cuts, and lips split and crusted.

She had risen from the black waters that night like something reborn and undone.

The sea had returned her.

But it had kept Eomma and Abeoji.

Now the water was quiet again, as if complicit, its dark secrets folded gently beneath the tides.

Since that day, she had survived on what others on the shore discarded without thought.

Soggy ramen crumbs clumped in greasy plastic cups. A half-eaten triangle gimbap, its seaweed peeling, the rice crusted and pecked at by gulls. A juice box, dented, its straw still sticky with the last film of syrup. A crinkled candy wrapper holding on to a few stubborn grains of sugar.

No one saw her.

No one called her name.

She didn't have one anymore.

Then today, while foraging near the rocks, she heard it—

The sudden peal of laughter, high and bright.

The unmistakable sound of children.

Their voices getting closer.

She froze, crouching deeper into her shadowed crevice at sea level where the breakwater met the cliff, her heart pounding like a cornered animal.

It was a quiet, remote stretch of shoreline, tucked away from the crowds, set apart from the busier parts of the beach farther down the coast.

She heard the laughter again—pure and full, bubbling with joy.

Like something from *Rainbow Family*,

Her favorite show from a life that now felt like someone else's.

Carefully, she leaned forward, squinting into the sunlight, trying to trace the laughter's source.

There—on the beach.

A family sprawled on a blanket, sunlight draping them in gold. A mother and two children, a little girl and a slightly older boy, sat cross-legged on a strawberry-pink blanket, its corners gently fluttering in the breeze like petals in bloom.

The little girl wore a white cotton dress dotted with tiny red hearts, her hair tied in uneven pigtails with pink bands.

Beside her, her brother crouched in black shorts and a tilted bucket hat, his limbs streaked with sand and salt as he molded and sculpted a small castle with quiet focus.

Their mother sat with her face shaded beneath the curve of a wide straw sun visor. She looked graceful and slender, clad in a pale blue linen blouse and a flowing white skirt, its hem dusted with sand. Her long black hair flowed freely, the wind teasing loose strands that danced around her face.

With quiet care, she unpacked their meal: triangular kimbap wrapped in crinkled plastic, peeled hard-boiled eggs, sliced peaches, and small cartons of banana milk.

The sight of food made her stomach ache with want. She imagined crawling close, unseen, and snatching a piece of kimbap before they noticed.

Just then the woman lifted her head. And her face came into full view—and for a second, the hunger faded.

Something about the woman's face—

The curve of her cheekbone, the delicate arch of her brows, the way the sunlight caught the fine lines around her mouth when she smiled—

Just like Eomma.

The same soft jawline, the same faint dimple that appeared only when she laughed.

Her skin was pale and smooth, glowing in the golden light, and her eyes—honey-warm and gentle—gazed at her children with a kind of quiet devotion.

Just like Eomma.

Even the way she lifted her hand to brush the hair from her daughter's forehead mirrored a gesture etched deep in her memory that felt familiar.

Her throat tightened.

The little girl clung to her side.

"Eomma," the child said—and giggled.

That single word shattered something deep inside her.

Like a spell summoning memories and emotions she thought had died.

Things she'd buried with the sea…

Now clawing their way back to the surface.

She couldn't move.

Couldn't look away.

The woman stood, brushing sand from her legs. She turned to the boy.

"Yejun-ah, dongsaeng jom bwajwo."

(Yejun, watch your sister.)

"Arasseo," the boy replied without looking up.

(Okay.)

But the moment she walked away, his gaze returned to the sandcastle, his fingers carving careful ridges into its towers, oblivious to everything else.

The little girl tugged on her brother's sleeve.

"Oppa, mul gaja!" she said.

(Older brother, let's go to the water!)

"Jom man. Na jigeum bappa," he muttered, eyes still on his sandcastle as he brushed her off.

(Just a sec. I'm busy right now.)

She waited a moment longer, eyes lingering on him—hopeful.

But when it was clear he wouldn't look her way, she turned quietly and drifted off.

One barefoot step. Then another.

Drawn to the sea's soft lullaby, she wandered toward the shimmering tide, giggling, eyes sparkling with delight, as if answering a secret call.

She stepped into the surf.

Ankle-deep.

Then knee-deep.

Farther still.

No one saw. No one but her.

Tucked in her hiding place, she waited—and watched.

Would someone come to save the little girl?

A heartbeat passed.

Then another.

Still no one noticed. No one moved.

The little girl was too deep now, as she struggled to stay afloat—

Thrashing, her arms flapping like broken wings.

She knew then: it was up to her.

She moved with quiet purpose. Her limbs slid into the water, the current curling around her like an old friend.

The waves welcomed her as if recognizing something long lost. As if they had been waiting.

Cold slid over her skin, gripped her bones—but she did not shiver.

Her body moved with strange grace, fluid and sure, as if the sea remembered her shape.

Then she dove.

And the world above dissolved into silence.

Beneath the surface, her arms cut cleanly through the water, Steady and certain.

From the shore, the mother noticed the girl missing.

She turned to the boy, her voice sharp with alarm.

"Eodi isseo? Jihye eodi gasseo?"

(Where is she? Where did Jihye go?)

The boy looked up, confused.

"Mollayo... banggeumkkaji yeogi isseosseo."

(I don't know... she was just here.)

Her eyes widened.

"Neo-ga jom bwajwo-ra-go haetjana!"

(I told you to watch her!)

Then she saw them—

Delicate footprints in the sand, leading straight into the water.

She froze.

"Jihye?" her voice rose in panic.

More frantic now: "JIHYE!"

Drawn by the mother's screams, people came running from the busier end of the beach, scanning the water in alarm.

"*Jeogi!*" someone shouted, pointing.

(There!)

"*Aiga isseo!*"

(There's a child!)

"*Hai-ga deo isseo! Du myeong-iya!*"

(There's another one! There are two!)

The little girl turned toward the older girl, eyes wide—

A flicker of recognition… or maybe hope.

And then under the surface—

In the muffled hush below the waves—

The older one reached out and gripped the child's waist.

Not to save.

But to silence.

"*Biane . . .*"

(I'm sorry.)

The little girl thrashed.

Tiny fingers clawed at the water.

Whimpers bubbled up, gurgles of confusion and terror.

The older girl's hand pressed down—

Gently, steadily, against the little girl's chest.

"Shhh," she whispered,

The way Eomma used to say when lulling her to sleep.

Then came silence.

A hush.

A lull.

And after a few minutes—

Stillness.

When it was over, she cradled the limp body in her arms and began to swim back—

Slowly, beautifully, like a savior returning from battle.

A saint bearing a sacrifice.

From a distance, it must have looked like a rescue

She emerged from the water like a vision—

Serene, glowing, almost holy.

The child's body floated beside her.

She let it drift—just far enough to seem accidental.

Then she collapsed onto the sand, eyes closed, limbs slack.

The crowd surged forward.

Gasps. Shouts.

Someone shouted, "119 *bureojwo!*"

(Call an ambulance!)

"*Sal-a isseo?*" another voice cried.

(Are they alive?)

The little one didn't stir.

But the older one did.

Her lashes fluttered—just barely.

The mother stumbled forward through the crowd,

Drawn to the small, still body on the sand.

She stopped a few feet away and stared.

As if her mind couldn't make sense of what her eyes were seeing.

She fell to her knees beside her daughter—

Hands trembling, reaching,

not ready to touch, not ready to know.

Then her sob rose—raw and unrestrained—a cry that could

split the world in two.

Her eyes went wild with disbelief and grief—

Until she heard it.

A voice. Small. Fragile.

"Eomma...?"

The girl's first word in years.

The mother froze.

Then slowly, she turned to face the other girl.

And in that fog of heartbreak, in that wild disorienting blur of grief,

Something inside her shifted.

"Jihye?" she gasped, the name catching in her throat like a lifeline.

The girl reached out blindly, trembling hesitating for just a moment—

Then folded into the woman's arms,

Pressing herself into the warmth her body still remembered.

Around them, murmurs bloomed:

"Eommani-rago han geon, heongnan ttaemune geuraetgetji."
   (*She must've called her "mom" because of the trauma.*)
   "Geu ai guhaetdago haejal manha."
   (*She tried to save the girl—they should be grateful.*)
   "Jigeum-eun swige hage haeya dwae. Gyeong jinja an pitda."
   (*She needs to rest now. Poor thing, she looks so pale.*)

No one questioned it.

Except one.

Just beyond the circle of awe stood the boy.

Silent. Still.

He watched the way the girl clung to his mother—too tightly.

203

The way she didn't cry.
The way her eyes flickered—not with grief,
But something else.
Something colder.
Hungrier.
He didn't understand it yet—not in words.
But somewhere deep inside him...
He knew.

[Fade to black as Lana Del Rey's "Once Upon a Dream" begins to play.]

End of Book One
Book Two—Coming October 31
Available for pre-order on Amazon.

Author Note

Thank you for reading, and for stepping into this world with me.

If you enjoyed *Death of an Idol*, I'd be incredibly grateful **if you left your review on Amazon and Goodreads**. Reviews make a huge difference in helping new readers discover the book—and as an indie author, your support truly means the world.

Death of an Idol began as a quiet question in the back of my mind—about memory, obsession, and the aching need to be seen and loved.

What started as a mystery slowly unfolded into something much more personal: a meditation on grief, identity, and the illusions we construct around love.

All the characters in this novel are Korean, and the story is set almost entirely in Korea. As a non-Korean author, writing a book so deeply rooted in a culture not my own came with both responsibility and challenge. I knew from the start that it would require care, humility, and extensive research to do it justice.

At the same time, writing from outside the culture allows one to see everything with fresh eyes—free from preconceived notions, biases, or cultural boundaries. It gave me the freedom and space to approach the world of this story without pressure, and with both empathy and objectivity.

From the intricate dynamics of Korean families to the unrelenting pressures of the idol industry, I tried my best to write with honesty and respect. I'm deeply grateful to my Korean friends and colleagues who offered their insight—especially around language, setting, and emotional nuance.

While I've taken some creative liberties, every choice was made with the hope and intention of honoring the complexity and beauty of Korea and its culture.

For the most part, all the dialogue between Korean characters in the book is imagined as being spoken entirely in Korean. However, since this is a novel in English for a global audience, I made some intentional decisions about when to preserve Korean phrasing, and when to translate into English to maintain clarity and flow. It's a delicate balance—and I hope readers will feel immersed in the world of my characters without ever getting lost in translation.

I'd love for you to **follow me** on my **YouTube channel** at youtube.com/@rimaraymysteries, where I share my reactions to K-pop songs—including many featured in the novel—as well as Korean and international films, shows, and series. You'll also find sneak peeks of upcoming books, exclusive giveaways, behind-the-scenes content, and book reviews of my favorite mystery novels—plus what's currently on my reading list. Most importantly, I hope to have the chance to chat and connect with you directly.

You can also find me on **Instagram** at instagram.com/rima_ray_author, where I'll be sharing my original sketches and short bios for all the major characters in *Death of an Idol*.

See you in the next one!

— Rima Ray

Glossary

If you're new to Korean language and culture, here are just a few words and phrases that appear throughout the book:

- **Eomma** – Mom
- **Abeoji** – Father (formal/polite)
- **Appa** – Dad (casual/intimate)
- **Halmeoni** – Grandmother
- **Harabeoji** – Grandfather
- **Hyung** – Older brother (used by males toward other males)
- **Noona** – Older sister (used by males toward older females)
- **Unni** – Older sister (used by females toward older females)
- **Majayo** – That's right / You're correct
- **Yeoboseyo** – Hello (used specifically when answering the phone)
- **Biane** – A soft, informal way of saying "I'm sorry" (often used between close friends or younger people)
- **Annyeonghaseyo** – A polite and common way to say "Hello"
- **Kamsahamnida** – A formal way of saying "Thank you"
- **Gomawo** – Informal way of saying "Thanks" (casual; between friends)
- **Jinjja** – Really / seriously (*used to express surprise, disbelief, or emphasis*)

- **Gwenchana** – "It's okay" or "I'm fine" (*used to reassure or comfort someone*)
- **Jebal** – Please (*often used in begging or urgent situations*)
- **Oppa** – Older brother (*used by females*; also can mean boyfriend in romantic contexts)
- **Noona** – Older sister (*used by males*)
- **Aigoo** – An exclamation like "Oh no," "Oh dear," or even a sigh of frustration/exhaustion
- **Hwaiting** – A Korean-English word of encouragement, like "You got this!" or "Let's go!"
- **Ajumma** – A middle-aged woman; commonly used to refer to or address women who are not relatives, similar to "auntie"
- **Ajussi** – A middle-aged man; commonly used to refer to or address men who are not relatives, similar to "uncle"

Acknowledgments

This story would not exist in its final form without the generous support, time, and encouragement of so many wonderful people.

To Jaeyong—thank you for being the very first reader of this manuscript. Your insights into Korean dialogue and cultural context were invaluable, and they gave me confidence in the authenticity of the characters and the world I was building.

To Sofia—thank you for patiently reading through every chapter and offering helpful notes. I really appreciate it.

A special shoutout to Patrick, currently serving in the Korean military, who still found time to reply despite having only one hour of internet access each week—that meant a lot. And I'll hold you to that promise to read the book when you can.

To Rachel, my editor and champion from my very first novel—you continue to believe in my voice and vision, and for that I'm endlessly grateful.

To Fred, who's been there from the inception of this idea for this novel to the final execution—thank you for reading drafts, weighing in on plot twists, and offering your unwavering support through it all. I couldn't have done it without you.

To my parents, who called every day just to check in and cheer me on from the Philippines—thank you for your love and faith in me.

To Kilho, my best friend, who still carved out time to

read chapters and share thoughtful feedback despite a hectic schedule in Korea—thank you for being there.

To Emily and Chris, my friends—thank you for reading the early prologue, showing interest, and encouraging me along the way.

To Stephanie Soo, whose true crime storytelling—especially of cases rooted in Asia—inspired me to craft my own Asian crime narrative.

To David Kim and Danny Kim, whose Youtube podcast was among the earliest sources that sparked my interest in Korean culture.

Last but definitely not least, thank you to Cha Eunwoo and IU, who served as the visual and emotional inspirations for my protagonists, Tae and Hana.

From my heart to yours—thank you all.

About the Author

Rima Ray is a bestselling Asian Canadian-American author and professor. She's a Reader's Digest and Amazon # 1 bestselling writer of mysteries and thrillers. Her debut novel won the Readers' Favorite Award in 2022.

She spent her childhood growing up around the world across nine different schools in seven different countries—Japan, Kuwait, Qatar, India, the Philippines, Canada and the US.

A survivor of both the First Gulf War in Kuwait and the 2011 triple disaster in Japan, Rima brings her global perspective to her stories.

These days she leads a more peaceful life crafting psychological mysteries and twisty thrillers from her home in Pittsburgh.

When not plotting her next novel, Rima enjoys reading, savoring Asian cuisine, and learning languages—she currently speaks four and is studying Korean and Japanese. She lives with her family, which includes her two cats, Million and Nobel, and her dog Mira—who act like they own the place (because they absolutely do).

Make sure to follow Rima on YouTube at @rimaraymysteries

for reactions to K-pop, Korean and international film and show, sneak peeks of upcoming books, giveaways, behind-the-scenes content, interactive Q&As, and much more.

You can also find her on Instagram at @rima_ray_author, where she shares character sketches and writing updates.

You can connect with me on:

🌐 https://www.youtube.com/@rimaraymysteries

🖉 https://www.instagram.com/rima_ray_author

Also by Rima Ray

Death of an Idol, Book 2 (Releasing 10/31)
The Explosive Conclusion to the K-Pop Psychological Mystery Thriller

PRE-ORDER now on Amazon!

He returned to Korea searching for answers. What he finds is a nightmare— an obsession disguised as love: twisted, relentless, and deadly.

From bestselling author, Rima Ray, comes the unforgettable and haunting conclusion to *Death of an Idol*, the addictive psychological thriller set in the dazzling and glamorous world of K-pop.

After the suspicious death of his fiancée on Jeju Island, Tae (Park Taejoon), former idol turned PhD student returns to Seoul—determined to uncover the truth. But some truths don't want to be found.

With former detective Yoon Hana by his side, Tae's investigation leads to a chilling truth: the deaths of his fiancée and Mino weren't isolated tragedies—they are connected. And carefully orchestrated by someone from Tae's past.

Someone who's been watching him for years. Someone who knows everything about him. Someone who would kill to become part of his life.

As the line between love and madness blur, Tae is forced to confront the twisted and terrifying obsession of someone who will stop at nothing to have him.

Love The Way You Die

From *Reader's Digest* Top 10 ranked mystery author and gifted storyteller comes a beautiful and original collection of romantic tales of mystery and suspense that navigate the themes of love, desire, guilt, loss and retribution.

A young attorney finds herself visiting a beautiful mansion inhabited by a reclusive older woman. A teenager remembers the events that transpired on her fifteenth birthday. A wife worries about her husband after hearing news of a devastating attack in her community. A newly married woman travels abroad to meet her spouse, hoping to make a fresh start and leave her dark past behind. A graduate student travails the unpredictable journey of falling madly in love and going through heartbreak.

Thrilling, suspenseful, poignant and innately human, the tales in this book make you experience all the nuances, shades, emotions and excesses of that mysterious and dangerous potion we call love. From the depths of unconditional sacrifice to the intensity of unfathomable hate, these stories invite you to come fall in love... *if you dare.*

Made in the USA
Columbia, SC
11 July 2025